Blackwater Swamp

Author: Wallace, Bill
Reading Level: 4.2
Point Value: 5.0
    ACCELERATED READER QUIZ # 11150

HER VOICE WAS SOFT, ALMOST A WHISPER.

"You no move. Da bear maybe sniff you. Maybe lick you. He maybe even put you arm in his mouth. You NO MOVE! Even if you hurt, you no move!"

Then . . .

She turned and walked away.

She left me there. The bear was so close I could see his shiny black nose. I could feel his breath on the back of my hand.

My lips were clamped tight around my teeth.

Even with my mouth shut, a little "squeak" came from my throat when his tongue stretched out to touch my bare arm. His tongue was as coarse and rough as driveway gravel.

I *knew* I was going to die.

And . . . the Witch of Blackwater Swamp simply walked off and left me for the bear.

Books by Bill Wallace

Red Dog
Trapped in Death Cave

Available from ARCHWAY Paperbacks

Beauty
The Biggest Klutz in Fifth Grade
Blackwater Swamp
Buffalo Gal
The Christmas Spurs
Danger in Quicksand Swamp
Danger on Panther Peak
(Original title: Shadow on the Snow)
A Dog Called Kitty
Ferret in the Bedroom, Lizards in the Fridge
Never Say Quit
Snot Stew
Totally Disgusting!
Watchdog and the Coyotes

Available from MINSTREL® Books

BLACKWATER SWAMP

BILL WALLACE

A MINSTREL® BOOK

PUBLISHED BY POCKET BOOKS

New York   London   Toronto   Sydney   Tokyo   Singapore

To the Priddles:
David, Dawn, Joshua, Jenny, and Katie

A Minstrel Book published by
POCKET BOOKS, a division of Simon & Schuster Inc.
1230 Avenue of the Americas, New York, NY 10020

Copyright © 1994 by Bill Wallace

Published by arrangement with Holiday House, Inc.

ISBN: 0-671-51156-4

First Minstrel Books printing April 1995

10 9 8 7 6 5 4 3 2

A MINSTREL BOOK and colophon are registered trademarks of Simon & Schuster Inc.

Cover art by Dan Burr

Printed in the U.S.A.

BLACKWATER SWAMP

CHAPTER
1

They say she came from Jamaica. She lived in the swamp. No one lived in the swamp—only her. They say she knew voodoo. They say she was a witch.

She was old and black as the night, with hair white and free as a cloud. How old she really was, how old she really looked, no one knew. She came in the night so she was never seen except in shadows.

Without a sound, she searched and scavenged the trash cans behind the restaurant along the bayou. And like a shadow she moved quietly, almost invisibly, from one place to the next.

What treasures she found, no one knew. Food, probably. I thought it sad that someone should have to scavenge like that, just to survive.

But the older boys at school said she wasn't

searching for food. "She hunts for things to add to that big, black pot where she mixes her magic brews. If you mess with her, she'll put a curse on you. After she finds things that belong to you, things you throw away, she knows how to get you."

I stayed clear of her. I stayed clear of the path that led away from the bridge to her house in the swamp.

I was waiting for my friend Don when I saw her. She came out of the trees on the riverbank and struggled up the terrace toward the cement bridge. The riverbank wasn't all that steep, but down here the land is so flat they have to pile dirt up before they can even build a road. The man-made hills they make are even higher, so rivers won't wash out a bridge when it rains. They look like little mountains on either side of a stream. It took her some time to cross the drainage ditch and make the climb. She paused a second and seemed to glance in my direction.

The breath caught in my throat. I pressed myself against one of the three cedar beams that supported the roof of our porch. I didn't wiggle. The slightest movement might give me away. She might turn. She might see me. I didn't even blink.

Before, I thought the Witch of Blackwater Swamp

was just a legend—a scary tale that the big kids at school made up to frighten little children.

Now that I had really seen her, I wasn't so sure.

At the edge of the road, she paused behind a clump of tall grass. A mosquito hummed in my ear. I didn't swat at it. She appeared again, after a moment, and walked across the bridge. Still stooped, she crept like some predator sneaking up on its prey. I felt the mosquito touch the fine hair on my earlobe. I left it alone.

On the other side of the bridge, she slipped quietly across the drainage ditch and into the trees. A chill raced up my back.

It wasn't more than a hundred yards from our porch to the far edge of the bridge. Still, within seconds, she was gone from my sight. Whether she disappeared through the pine trees, or whether the evening light and her dark clothing and even darker skin made it impossible for me to see her, I wasn't sure. It didn't matter either. The mosquito hummed off. It itched where I'd been bit on my ear. I didn't scratch.

I took a deep breath. I could hardly wait for Don to get here so I could tell him I had really seen her. The Witch of Blackwater Swamp wasn't just a figure in a fairy tale. She was real. She looked just the way the kids at school had described her.

There was still enough light to see, but it was darker now. The sounds of bugs zooming and whooshing and zinging filled the evening air. Bullfrogs bellowed from the swamp behind our house.

Two years ago, we lived in a white, frame house at the edge of a little town called Chickasha in Oklahoma. Not far from the house was a pond. It had bullfrogs that croaked. Little bullfrogs croak, but big bullfrogs, like the ones here in Louisiana, bellow.

Two years before moving to Chickasha, we lived in Wyoming. Wyoming didn't have bullfrogs, at least not where we lived. There weren't many bugs in Wyoming either. The mayflies were pretty. 'Course, some of the mosquitoes were as big as horseflies. Houston, where we lived before coming here, had everything—especially traffic.

Seems like the bugs, the bridges, and the heat were what I noticed most when we moved to Louisiana. If I left something out in the yard, within a day or two, something would crawl under it and tote it off. I'd never seen so many bugs.

The heat was another thing. In Wyoming I had to sleep under a blanket, even in the summertime. If it ever got to ninety, people thought they were having a heat wave and wouldn't go out. In Oklahoma, if it got to ninety in August, folks called it a cool front and rushed outside to enjoy the nice weather.

In Wyoming, I looked forward to summer. Here, I was dreading the thought. It was April and already the days were in the eighties. I couldn't imagine what August would be like. Well . . . I could. I just didn't want to.

More bugs hummed. More bullfrogs joined the bellowing chorus behind the house. The shadows no longer crept across the yard. They raced over the ground like clouds sweeping through a stormy sky. My eyes never left the place where the old lady had disappeared into the trees. I could see the darkness. I could feel it all around me.

I spun around, yanked the screen door open, and slipped inside. Once there, I wheeled back and closed the screen behind me. I held the handle and flipped the little hook into the latch.

I could watch for Don just as well from inside.

CHAPTER
2

The thing I hate most about moving all the time is not having any pets. I love animals. When I was real little, I had a turtle. After that I had a dog named Toy, but when he died, Mama said we didn't need another one. She said it was too hard to haul a dog or cat all over the country with us.

I wish we could stay put for a while. I wish I could have another dog like Toy. But Daddy says when you work in the oil patch, it's either feast or famine. What that means is that when the oil business is good, everything's great. We have lots of money and can do lots of stuff.

When the oil business is off, like it has been for the last eight years, we have to move a lot. Daddy has changed jobs and got laid off and found new jobs. Sometimes the oil companies he has worked for have folded up. They've gone out of business or gone broke and he's had to find a new bunch of people to work for.

Daddy's an engineer. He went to college and is pretty smart, as far as dads go. We studied about engineers in school in Oklahoma. But he's not the kind of engineer that builds bridges or tall buildings. He's what's called a petroleum engineer. That doesn't mean he builds oil wells either. It means he knows a whole bunch about rocks and stuff, like what kind of rocks you find near oil that's down deep in the ground.

Besides not having any pets because of moving, I've also had problems making friends. Just about the time I've started to make good friends at a school, my family's taken off and gone someplace else. Seems like I'd be good at making new friends, as much as we've moved. I guess I am. I loved Wyoming. After the first couple of weeks, I liked Oklahoma, too. Then we moved to Houston. It only took me a couple of days to find some new friends there. Our school was nice. The kids were friendly. Only, Daddy didn't like Houston traffic. Daddy grew up in a little town. He liked little towns. Houston *wasn't* a little town. He said it was too big and the traffic was *terrible*. So we moved to Lakeview, Louisiana.

I liked Houston. I didn't like Lakeview. After four months, the only friend I really had was Don Lyons. After four months, he was the first guy to come spend the night with me. Four months without having a best friend is a long time.

Mama said the people who lived in Lakeview lived there forever. They either knew everybody in town or they were related to everybody in town. It was one of those places where lots of people left, but not many new people moved in. That's why it was hard to make friends—people just weren't used to new folks coming to town.

Don was new in town, too. His dad was a dentist, and since the dentist who used to live in Lakeview died of a heart attack around Christmas, the Lyonses moved here then. Don said he'd never moved before. He didn't know how to make friends. "Besides," he told me, "when your dad's a dentist, it's hard making friends *anyplace*. Nobody likes dentists."

Don laughed when he told me that. But I think, in a way, he was kind of serious about what he said, too.

All the other guys in our fifth-grade class had people to run around with. All of them already had best friends. Don and I just sort of fell in together because nobody else wanted us.

Don and I didn't have much in common either. Don liked to read. I liked to watch TV. Don liked fishing. I liked playing football or basketball or riding my bicycle. Don didn't do much outdoors stuff—just fishing. He was all right, I guess. He was smart and fun to be with, just not very exciting.

Jimmy Weston was a lot more exciting than Don. Jimmy was sort of new in town, too. He and his mother had lived here before but had moved away. They had only been back two weeks before I moved here. I didn't know Jimmy that well. I'd probably ask him over to spend the night next, after Don.

Some lights shined on the bridge. I pressed my cheek against the screen, hoping it was Don. Then I heard the sound of tires squealing.

It wasn't Don.

The sound of an engine roared. The headlights swayed and bounced as the car raced across the bridge. The tires squealed again as the driver changed gears. He was driving a black '57 Chevy. It was a really sharp-looking car, too. The teenage guy who owned it kept it polished and shiny. Hard telling how much work he'd done on the motor to make it run like that. The thing sounded like a race car at the Indianapolis 500 as it sped past our house.

I glanced down when I felt something brush my leg. It was my sister Kristine. She stood on her tiptoes, trying to see out the bottom of the screen.

"Out."

She looked up at me. I looked down and shook my head.

"Out!" she repeated.

Then Mama was beside me. She picked up Kristine and looked through the screen.

"That kid in the black car again?"

I nodded. Mama made kind of a clucking sound and shook her head.

"Don't know why the police don't catch him. I know your father's reported the way he drives. He's probably related to the police somehow—one of their brothers or cousins or something. That kid's gonna kill somebody if he keeps driving like that." She made that clucking sound again and carried Kristine back to her playpen so she would be out of the way while Mama finished the dishes.

Another glow reflected off the side of the cement bridge. This car approached slowly. It turned into our driveway and stopped. I unlatched the screen, looked both ways—just to make sure the old witch hadn't come back—and stepped out on the porch to meet Don. I could hardly wait to tell him about the witch.

CHAPTER
3

"That's stupid," Don Lyons scoffed. "There's no such thing as witches."

My mouth scrunched up on one side.

"You should have seen her, man. I mean, you talk about creepy! She's got this long, wild, white hair. It goes all over the place. She sort of sneaks around, too. You know, crouches down and creeps in the shadows. And . . ."

"I've seen her in town," Don said. "We went out to eat at Donovan's, and when we came out, she was digging in the trash can by the parking lot." He got off the edge of my bed and went to look at the stuff on my dresser. "In Austin, where we lived before, there're street people. I used to think they were only in big towns like Dallas or New York or Los

Angeles, but they're all over. Lakeview is just a little tiny place. Since it's so little, instead of having a bunch of street people, it only has one. She's it. That doesn't make her a witch."

Feeling a little disgusted with him, I sighed.

"But street people don't have a home. She does. It's out in the swamp. Nobody lives in a swamp, nobody but a witch."

Don pulled a couple of books from the top of my dresser.

"You read this one?" he asked, holding up a copy of *Kidnapping Kevin Kowalski* by Mary Jane Auch.

I shook my head. "No. But if she isn't a witch, why would she . . ."

"Oh, this is a fantastic adventure," he said. He turned around and showed me the cover of Cynthia DeFelice's *Weasel*. "You've read that one, haven't you?"

I shrugged. "Most of it. I had to do a book report on it, but I faked the ending since I didn't have time to read all of it." I cleared my throat. "But, like I was saying, how would all those stories get started about her being a witch if there wasn't some truth to it?"

"Golly," Don yelped. "You got an autographed copy of *Scared Stiff*." He waved the book at me. "I can't believe it! Man, that Willo Davis Roberts is a great writer. How'd you ever get an autographed copy of her book?"

I wanted to talk about the scary, old witch I'd seen. Don wanted to talk about my books. Don was company. Besides, he wasn't listening to me, anyway, so . . .

"She came to visit the school I went to in Houston," I answered.

"My favorite book of hers is *The View from the Cherry Tree*. Is this one your favorite?"

I shrugged. "I don't know. I haven't read it yet."

Don's mouth flopped open and his chin almost dropped to the floor.

"You haven't read it? How come you picked it?"

I shrugged again. "Everybody else was getting books for her to autograph, so I figured I would, too. Got that one 'cause the picture on the front looked interesting."

Don shook his head. He closed the book gently and put it back on my dresser.

I cocked an eyebrow. "We could play with some of my video games. How about watching TV?"

"All these neat books and you haven't read them?" Don sighed.

"Maybe tomorrow we could go out in the swamp and spy on the old witch."

Don only shook his head again. "Can't believe you don't read."

Monday, in the school lunchroom, Jimmy Weston looked at me over the peach half he had stuck on the end of his fork like a lollipop.

"Don sounds like a real nerd to me."

I kind of laughed and shook my head.

"Nah. He's all right. Well . . . the evening was kind of boring. He read some of my books while I watched TV. But in the morning, after Mama made us pancakes for breakfast, we went out and threw the football some. Don's got a pretty good throwin' arm. Then we played catch with my baseball and . . ."

"But did you ever get to the swamp?" Jimmy cut me off. "Did you ever find her house?"

I sighed and shook my head again.

"No. Don told me that his dad wouldn't let him go into the swamp, not unless he was with him. So we just hung around the yard and did stuff."

Jimmy shrugged. "Like I said, a real nerd."

He crammed the peach half into his mouth and said something. With all the commotion in the lunchroom, it was almost impossible to hear. With

Jimmy trying to talk around a mouthful of peach . . .

"What?" I frowned.

Jimmy chomped a couple of times, then swallowed. The lump that went down his long, skinny neck was so big, he reminded me of a snake swallowing a frog.

"I said, I woulda gone with you."

I cocked my head to the side. "Huh?"

"The swamp. I woulda gone with you in a second. All you got to say is 'Let's go.' We'd find that old witch's house. We'd sneak up and watch her and . . ."

"You really mean it?" I gasped. "Really?"

"Sure." Jimmy shrugged. "You know, my cousin Bubba has seen her house. He told me about it once. He said it's about a mile from that bridge, and he used to sneak out there and spy on her when he was little. Why don't we do it? Why don't we see if we can find her house?"

I finished chewing before answering him. (Mama always told me not to talk with my mouth full.)

"Who's Bubba?"

"My cousin."

"But what's his real name?"

"That is his real name. Bubba. Bubba Larkin. He's in high school. And he's been out in that swamp a lot. Bubba's seen her place. Says it looks more like a shack than a house, but he's seen it. If he was able to find it, we could, too. Wanna go?"

"Sure," I answered, "if you want to."

"How about this afternoon?"

I took a sip of milk.

"Can't."

"Why not?"

"Mama won't let me run around on a school day."

"None at all?"

I wiped the milk from my lips with the back of my hand. "Well, for a couple of hours right after school. But if the old lady's house is really a mile out in the swamp, it might take us more than an hour or two to get there and back. Hard telling what kind of brush and mud or stuff like that we might have to walk through. I mean, walking in a swamp is lots harder than just walking down a sidewalk or something. Besides, by the time we got out there it'd be almost dark. I don't want to be out in that swamp when it's dark."

Jimmy's eyebrows shot up. "Yeah. Me neither. But you say your mom lets you play around a couple of hours after school?"

I nodded.

"You got a bike?"

I nodded again.

Jimmy bit on his thin bottom lip. "Why don't you

ride over to Parsons' Grocery after school today? That's about halfway between your house and mine. We can get us a soft drink and either ride over to Connors or the park and mess around a while."

"What's Connors?"

"It's kind of a hangout. It's where Bubba and a bunch of the guys sit around and talk and stuff."

Hanging around with a bunch of high-school guys didn't sound like much fun. "How about the park?" I suggested.

"Fine," Jimmy said. "There're lots of trails for our bikes and jumps and stuff to do."

"Sounds good."

"Oh, by the way," he said as we walked toward the lunchroom door, "you get your math homework done this weekend?"

"Yeah."

"You mind if I borrow it? We had a bunch of stuff to do. I didn't have time to get mine done."

I wanted to go out and play. Don told me that some kids from his homeroom were gonna have a softball game at noon recess. Instead, I went back to my room and got my math assignment for Jimmy.

Ordinarily I didn't like loaning guys my homework. For some reason it just didn't seem right. But since Jimmy and I were going to ride our bikes and mess around in the park, since we were going to start being good friends . . . well . . .

"I'll get it back to you before class," Jimmy said, snatching the paper from my hand. "Promise."

Jimmy kept his promise. I worried about it most of the afternoon. But right as we were going into sixth-hour math class, Jimmy met me at the door and handed me my assignment. "See you at Parsons' Grocery about four."

CHAPTER
4

Mr. Parsons was a short little squatty man. He had white hair, red cheeks, and a smile that wouldn't quit. Mama usually did her grocery shopping at the big I.G.A. store downtown. We'd been into Parsons' a few times, though, when she'd forgotten something or when she just had a few things to buy and didn't want to drive to the I.G.A.

"Hi, Ted," he greeted when I walked in, "your mom doing okay?"

I smiled, amazed that he remembered my name. Then I nodded. "She's fine, Mr. Parsons. Kristine's keeping her real busy. That's why we haven't been in."

"That Kristine's a little doll. Anything I can help you with?"

I shook my head. "No. Just waiting for a friend. We're gonna get us a soft drink, then go over and play around in the park."

Mr. Parsons motioned at the big trash can near the cash register. I could see some cans buried in the ice that almost spilled over the top of the thing.

"Don't know what kind of drink you want, but these are good 'n' cold. They're on sale, too."

Behind me, I heard the door squeak. I glanced over my shoulder and saw Jimmy. He smiled and waved. "Hi, Ted. Mr. Parsons."

Mr. Parsons nodded. "Hi, Jimmy," he responded, only his smile wasn't as big as when he greeted me and he didn't ask about Jimmy's family.

I didn't think much about it, not at the time. I was ready to head off to the park. I dug around in the ice until I found a strawberry soda. My hand was so cold it hurt. I put the soft drink on the counter and knocked off the pieces of ice that stuck to my skin.

When I paid Mr. Parsons, he didn't really look at me. He kind of kept stretching up, trying to see over the display racks. I figured that someone else had come into the store and he was seeing if they needed help or something. He gave me my change. I thought about getting a candy bar or some peanuts—I was always a little hungry right after school.

But I'd only brought a dollar, and I didn't have enough change to get anything else. Instead, I reached in and pulled out two pieces of bubble gum from a plastic jar near the cash register. I paid for them, took my change and the gum, and stuffed them into my pocket.

Jimmy came from the back of the store. He had a strawberry soda. It was a different brand than the one I got out of the ice bucket, but it was still strawberry.

"These are on sale," I said, pointing at the bucket. "They're really cold too."

Jimmy's lip sort of curled.

"Nah. This is the kind I like."

He paid Mr. Parsons, and we got our bikes. About two blocks from the store, Jimmy pulled over to the side of the road. I stopped my bike beside him.

"Want a candy bar?" He reached into his pocket.

I frowned, looking at the two Snickers he held out to me.

"I didn't see you get those," I said, almost thinking out loud. "Did you pay for them?"

Jimmy shrugged. "No."

I tilted my head to the side. My eyes felt tight.

Jimmy cleared his throat. His lips seemed even thinner than usual.

"Brought 'em from home. Mama always keeps some in the refrigerator for me to have after school." He stuck them closer to my face. "You want one or not?"

"Sure."

I took the Snickers bar and started unwrapping it. Jimmy stuck the edge of his wrapper in his mouth like he was going to tear it open. Then, with one leg, he jumped down hard on his bicycle pedal.

"Race you to the park!" he called over his shoulder. "Last one there's a rotten egg!"

So I was a rotten egg. Big deal.

There was no way I could beat Jimmy. First off, I had my hands full of candy wrapper. He had sort of tricked me and had such a head start, I didn't stand a chance. Second, I wasn't even sure where the park was, much less where we were going once we got there.

It bothered me a little that Jimmy kind of cheated me. But it was no big deal. After I followed him to the park, we stopped and lifted our bikes over a short rock wall that surrounded a lake. There was a cement plaque stuck in the rock. It said, W.P.A. 1936.

Between the wall and the pond was some playground equipment. There were about three merry-go-rounds, a couple of big Ferris wheel things, and some swings. We stopped and played on the stuff for a while.

Then Jimmy got on his bike and rode around the lake to the top of the dam. I followed him to a couple of rest rooms on the far side. We found the one marked Men and went in. But instead of leaving after we'd gone to the bathroom, Jimmy started yanking toilet paper off the rolls and throwing it into the pots.

Guys back at the school I went to in Houston used to do that sometimes. I always figured it wasn't right. Besides, if I ever did stuff like that, with my luck I'd get caught. So while Jimmy trashed the bathroom, I went out and sat on my bike.

We rode back across the dam and chased the ducks for a while. It was fun. We'd get close to them with our bikes, and they'd go waddling off toward the water. They'd quack and squawk and flap their wings. I couldn't help but marvel at how dumb and clumsy they looked on the ground, yet how smooth and graceful they were once they got in the water.

We laughed and rode through the waddling herd over and over. Then, Jimmy hit one. He didn't hurt it. The duck rolled over, jumped right up on his feet again, and didn't even limp much when he raced for the pond.

I love animals. I don't like it much when somebody tries to hurt them or be mean to them. But I didn't think Jimmy tried to hit the thing on purpose.

Then the next time we rode through, he kicked at one with his foot. He missed and only knocked out a couple of white tail feathers. It was enough to take the fun out of our little game.

There were only a few ducks left on the bank. Jimmy wanted to ride at them once more, but I suggested we go play on the swings awhile.

"That's little-kid stuff," he scoffed. "Let's go get them ducks. Bet I can hit that old fat one over there."

I glanced at my watch. It was ten minutes to five. I didn't have to be home until five-thirty, but I turned my bike and headed for the rock wall.

"Getting late," I called over my shoulder. "Got to get home."

I was glad Jimmy followed me instead of trying to hurt the ducks. When I stopped at the rock wall, he pulled up beside me.

"You didn't get to stay long." He pouted. "What time you gotta be home?"

"Around five." I lied—well it wasn't really a lie.

Five-thirty *was* around five. And leaving was the only way I figured I could get Jimmy away from the ducks. "Why? What time you gotta be home?"

Jimmy shrugged.

"Mama goes to the bar at five. She don't know when I get home."

I tilted my head. "Your mom goes to the bar?"

Jimmy smiled. "Yeah. She waits tables and stuff. Anyway, she don't know when I get home, so I can stay out as late as I want and tell her I got home at five or five-thirty. Whatever I feel like."

He nodded toward the ducks. "You want to come back tomorrow?"

I shook my head.

"No. Got a book report due for Mrs. Dobie's class on Friday, and I haven't even started reading a book yet. Better do that."

"Old 'Dopey Dobie.'" Jimmy made a snorting sound. "She's so old and dumb she won't know whether you read a book or not. Just make up stuff. Fake it."

I lifted my bicycle over the rock wall.

"No. I'm not the best reader in the world, but I'm even worse at faking book reports. I tried that once when we lived in Oklahoma. I think I better read the book."

Jimmy just shrugged. He lifted his bike over the wall, and we left the park (and the ducks).

We stopped at the corner in front of Parsons' Grocery. Jimmy got off his bike.

"Want another drink?"

I shook my head. "No. Don't have enough money left."

Jimmy patted his pocket. "I always got plenty of money. I'll buy you one if you want."

"No thanks." I took a deep breath. "While we were riding back up here," I began, "I got to thinking about the old witch. You know, down in the swamp? You want to spend the night Saturday and see if we can find her house?"

Jimmy's eyes lit up. Then his shoulders sort of sagged, and he shook his head.

"Can't. Something I got to do Saturday evening."

"What?"

"Supposed to help Mom around the house and stuff."

I tilted my head to the side.

"I thought you said your mom went to work at five."

Jimmy gave a little jerk. "Ah . . . er . . . ," he stammered. "Well, it's her day off, and I promised I'd help her."

"Your mom works at a bar and she gets Saturdays off?" My mouth flopped open, and I had to push it shut with my hand. "Thought bars were real busy on Saturdays."

"Well, she usually works on Saturdays." Jimmy didn't look at me. "Just this Saturday that she's off. I could come over on Friday night. We could go out there Saturday morning. My cousin could drop me off Friday on his way to Shreveport. Should be about five or six."

"All right!"

CHAPTER
5

After school on Friday, Mama wanted me to stop by Parsons' Grocery on the way home to get Kristine some milk. I was in such a hurry, I almost ran into one of the teacher's cars.

I don't know why I was in such a rush. Mr. Parsons was talking to some guy when I came in. He smiled and waved, then kept right on talking.

I dug in my pocket and pulled out the wad of money that Mama had given me. There was a little note held to the dollar bills with a paper clip. I unfolded it.

Velveeta Cheese
½ gallon milk
1 can water-based tuna (large)
1 candy bar (whatever you want)
　　　Love,
　　　Mama

I couldn't help smiling when I read it. I gathered all the items on the list as quickly as I could, then trotted back to where Mr. Parsons leaned against the cash register.

He was *still* talking.

". . . And what all did they take?"

The man standing across the counter from him shrugged. "Sheriff Thibodeaux is working on it. So far, they know they're missing about ten cases of beer, whatever change was left in the cash register, and some bottles of whiskey."

Mr. Parsons shook his head. "They'll probably have to inventory the whole store. They bust the door or climb through a window?"

The other man folded his arms. "That's what's got the sheriff stumped. No windows busted, no marks on the door from somebody trying to pry open the lock. Nothing. The sheriff said the exact same thing happened at Jake's Jewelry about two weeks ago. Got a bunch of rings and necklaces and timepieces from the display cases, but they never could figure how the thief got in."

Mr. Parsons nodded, then pointed up at a metal grate on the wall behind him. "Had the same thing here, about three years back. Bunch of stuff stolen and no sign of any kind of break-in. Then that air vent fell off one day and darn near busted me on the head. Sheriff said the screws were stripped, and he climbed up and looked in the air-conditioner vent with his flashlight. Sure enough, the dust was messed up where somebody had crawled through it."

"Ever figure out who it was?"

Mr. Parsons shook his head. "No. But whoever it was musta been pretty small to squeeze through that vent."

I lifted the tuna can I'd set on the counter, then clunked it down again, hoping the noise would remind Mr. Parsons that I was there and ready to pay for my groceries.

It didn't work.

"Sheriff got any ideas about this one?" he asked the man.

I cleared my throat.

"Mr. Parsons?"

He kind of jumped. He looked at me with a sheepish smile.

"I'm sorry, Ted," he apologized. "I forgot you were standin' there. Got everything you need?"

"Yes sir," I answered as I shoved the wad of dollar bills toward him.

Mr. Parsons lifted each item and rang it up on the cash register. Then he counted the money and handed me some change.

"We were talking about the robbery over at Bird-well's Liquor Store. Lakeview ain't very big and anytime there's a break-in, it's news. Didn't mean to make you wait so long."

I smiled back at him.

"It's okay, Mr. Parsons," I lied. "I wasn't in any big rush." I picked up the sack he had put the things in and bolted for the door.

"Like I was saying"—I could hear Mr. Parsons start up again—"Sheriff got any leads or ideas about this round of robberies?"

The voices faded behind me. I jumped on my bicycle and tore off down the road. In my head, I started going over all the things I needed to do before Jimmy came over.

First off, I'd left my room in a mess. Mama was always fussing about my room. Mostly I kept stuff picked up pretty well, but I needed to straighten it before company came. Next, I needed to find my canteen in case Jimmy and I got thirsty when we explored the swamp tomorrow.

I held the sack tighter against my chest and ped-aled harder. My bike was really flying when I rounded the corner near our house. I was halfway across the bridge when I saw her.

The old woman was down on her knees at the side of the bridge.

I gasped, but the air stopped at the sudden lump that jumped into my throat. I grabbed the hand brake and squeezed. My tires squealed, leaving a thin trail of black rubber behind me. The sack of groceries fell from my hand. I grabbed the other brake.

The old woman raised her head and looked toward me.

There was a tiny pile of loose gravel on the bridge. I hit it. The bike slid. I went down. My left leg stung as it scraped the cement. Still straddling the bike, but lying on my left side, I slid to a stop.

Not ten feet from where I lay, the old woman struggled to her feet. She glared at me with dark eyes.

It was the witch. The Witch of Blackwater Swamp.

CHAPTER
6

It was broad daylight. I'd only seen her once, and that had been in the evening. Evening—that's when people talked about her. That's when they said she came from the swamp. I never dreamed she would be here. I never expected her—not now!

I couldn't seem to move. I was frozen, one leg trapped beneath my bicycle. The witch picked up something from the ground. I couldn't tell what it was. She looked at me one last time.

She was as old as the river itself. From where I was lying, I could see her wrinkles. They made her face look scarred and angry. Her withered hands were gnarled and twisted like the limbs of a mountain cedar whipped by an angry wind.

She tucked whatever she'd picked up from the

bridge against her chest. Then, with her arms wrapped around her "treasure," she turned and scurried away. She went down the side of the bridge toward the riverbank.

She moved on shuffling feet, with her shoulders and back slumped low like the weeping willows that lined the shady banks. The last thing I saw was the top of her head as it disappeared below the cement bridge rail.

I don't know how long I lay there. Finally, a little voice inside my head said: "You're in the middle of the road, stupid. Get up!" Kicking my right leg, I shoved the bicycle off me and struggled to my feet.

I raced to the side of the bridge, then stopped and cautiously peeked over.

The witch was far down the path. Still clutching the thing she had picked up from the bridge, she rounded a bend in the riverbank and vanished beyond some tall trees.

It was then that I felt the pain where my leg had scraped the concrete. My heart was pounding in my ears. My mouth was as dry as cotton. I ran my tongue over my lips and turned around to get my bike and the groceries.

When I'd dropped the sack, it had busted. The can of tuna and the Velveeta Cheese had landed clear on the far side of the bridge. One corner of the

cheese box was bent and the can was dented, but
they were okay. The carton of milk was near my
bike. One side was dirty, but it hadn't burst. The
M&M's I'd gotten for myself hadn't fared so well.
The little sack they'd come in had popped open and
M&M's were scattered all over the bridge. I left
them and picked up everything else.

After one last peek, to make sure the old witch
hadn't turned and come back in my direction, I got
my bike. As I walked it past the end of the bridge,
I paused to look where I'd seen the old woman
kneeling.

There was nothing there. I frowned and looked
around some more. That's when I saw it.

Blood.

A chill raced up my back. My knees trembled.

There were only two drops, but it was blood.
Dark and red, it caught my eye and shined up at me
like a flashlight shimmering through a dark night.

Pushing my bike, I *ran* for the house.

I could hardly wait to tell Mama. I'd seen the
Witch of Blackwater Swamp—I'd seen her up
close—and there was blood on the bridge. I
dropped my bicycle in the front yard and raced for
the screen door.

This was important! This was scary! I had to tell
somebody.

*   *   *

I never got the chance to tell Mama. She met me as I bounded up on the porch. Her chin jutted out as she glared at me.

"Where have you been, young man?" she demanded.

My tennis shoes squeaked when I slid to a stop.

"I . . . ah . . . ," I stammered.

"Well? You're supposed to come *straight* home after school and . . ."

I leaned to the side and glanced down at the milk, cheese, and tuna that I clutched against my chest.

"You told me to stop at Parsons'. Remember?"

Her angry glare softened.

"Oh."

I squeezed past her to get inside the house. "He was talking to some guy about a robbery. I had to wait on him. Then, when I was riding across the bridge, I almost ran into that old witch and . . ."

Even though I was well inside the house, Mama still stood, holding the screen open. She waved at me to be quiet.

"Not right now. I don't have time . . ."

"But, Mama," I protested. I just had to tell her what I'd seen. "I was riding across the bridge and . . ."

"NOT RIGHT NOW!" she roared, cutting me off.

My lips wrapped around my teeth, and I clamped my mouth shut. I could feel my eyes welling up.

Mama sighed. "I'm sorry, Ted," she said, still holding the screen open. "I didn't mean to yell at you. I forgot about sending you to the grocery store. I'm sorry, but I've got to go. I'll be right back and you can tell me . . ."

"But, Mama," I whined.

She shook her head.

"Whatever happened, you can tell me later. I lost a filling, and my tooth's killing me." She opened her mouth and stuck a finger way up inside. "I called Dr. Lyons and he said if I hurried, he'd wait for me." She grabbed her keys from her purse and let the screen bounce shut behind her. "Give Kristine some milk in her little cup with the top on it. You can fix yourself a tuna sandwich. There are chips in the pantry."

I went back to the front door. The screen felt cold against my nose. I watched Mama, still talking every step of the way to the car.

"It shouldn't take long," she said, grabbing the door handle. "You can tell me what happened on the bridge when I get home. Watch Kristine!"

She slammed the car door and drove off.

I stood with my nose pressed against the screen and my mouth open.

"Can't believe it," I moaned to myself. "Almost kill myself in a bicycle wreck, pick up the groceries that *she* told me to get, rip my leg up, find blood on the bridge, almost run smack over the old witch— and the *only* thing she has time to say to me is, 'WATCH KRISTINE!' "

My shoulders sagged. The can of tuna rolled from its resting place in my arm. It went clunk on the floor. The box of Velveeta went crunch.

"She doesn't even care," I grumbled. "She never listens to me. 'WATCH KRISTINE.' That's all she ever says."

Kristine was in her high chair. She smiled. Kristine was always happy to see me when I got home from school. I glared at her. She smiled even more and held her arms out toward me.

"Down." She grinned.

"Aw, shut up!"

CHAPTER
7

How I managed to get things together I still don't know. But I did.

I found Kristine's milk cup and poured her some milk. Then I opened the tuna can. The mayonnaise was hidden in the back of the fridge, but I finally dug it out. I put the tuna in a bowl, glopped some mayonnaise on it, and mixed up some tuna salad for a sandwich.

Mama had been so worried about her dumb tooth, she must have forgotten that Jimmy was coming over. I put the salad back in the refrigerator instead of fixing myself a sandwich. That way, there would at least be something for Jimmy to eat if he got here before Mama came back.

Even though Kristine's cup had a top, she managed to pour most of her milk onto the high chair. She kept holding out her arms and saying "Down."

Then she started crying.

I felt like a real heel for telling her to shut up. It wasn't Kristine's fault that Mama didn't care if I'd almost killed myself on my bicycle. It wasn't her fault that Mama dumped her on me either.

So after a while I picked her up and gave her a big hug and a kiss. Then I set her down beside her high chair.

She hugged me back and kissed me on the cheek. It was one of those sloppy kisses, all juicy from milk and spit. When you're a big brother, you get used to those kinds of kisses. I wiped it off, patted her on the bottom, and told her to go play with her toys. As she waddled off, I went to the pantry and dug around to see if there were any chips. A tuna sandwich wasn't much by itself. If I could find some chips to go with it . . .

"Out," I heard Kristine call from the other room.

I found the chips and put them on the counter by the refrigerator.

"Out!"

"No," I answered. "Play with your toys."

"Out!"

I got a couple of paper plates from the cupboard, then went back to the pantry and found two cans of

Coke. Looking things over one last time, I brushed my hands together. "Got stuff ready for supper," I told myself. "Now got to work on my room."

Kristine was waddling toward the front door as I walked through the living room.

"Come on and play with your toys, Kristine."

She pointed to the door.

"Out."

I went after her. I tucked her under my arm like a football and trotted toward my room.

"Out!" she protested.

Kristine's room was next to mine. I found her box of toys and dumped them out on the floor. Kristine always dumped stuff out, so I figured I'd save her the trouble. With my foot I made a bare spot in the middle of all the dolls and toy men and Weeble cars and people. I plopped her down in the middle and headed for my room.

"Play with your toys. I'll be back in a minute."

"Play Kristine?"

I shook my head. "Don't have time to play with Kristine right now. Later. You play by yourself."

"Out!"

I ignored her and started picking up stuff from my floor. Mama usually got on to me every three or four days for not cleaning my room. If I remembered, I tried to straighten stuff up every two days. That kept her from yelling at me. I must have forgotten, though, 'cause my room was a real pit.

There were socks all over the floor, underwear and T-shirts tossed in the corners, and a plate and fork under the bed. My nose wrinkled up as I remembered eating supper in here last Monday. I forgot to take the dirty dishes back to the kitchen and now it was Friday.

I pitched the socks and the rest of my clothes in a pile by the door. I stuck the plate and fork right in front of the door so I wouldn't forget them on my way out. Then I stacked my schoolbooks and notebook neatly on my desk. I straightened the pillows on my bed and tried to make it up. Mama always made my bed look smooth and neat when she fixed it. As I stepped back and looked at all the lumps and wrinkles, I frowned. Then, with a shrug I figured, "Maybe Jimmy won't notice."

It took both my arms and chin to control the pile of dirty clothes I carried to the laundry room. The dryer was tumbling and there was already stuff that had been washed lying in the washing machine. I stuffed my clothes in the pink wicker basket by the washer and went back to my room. I snatched the plate and fork from the doorway and trotted toward the kitchen.

It had taken me longer to get things straightened

up than I'd thought. I glanced at the clock in the living room. It was 6:05.

My room was clean—well, mostly clean. Stuff for supper was out and ready. Jimmy told me he'd be here by about five or six. Here it was, five after six, and he still wasn't here.

"Kristine, let's pick your toys up and go watch TV," I called.

Kristine wasn't sitting in the middle of her toys when I walked into her room.

I looked around. She wasn't hiding by the door. Or on the other side of her bed.

"Kristine? Where are you?"

I jabbed my fists against my hips and squinted.

"Kristine! I don't know where you're hiding, but you get out here, *right now*, and help me pick up your toys."

I held my breath and listened.

"Kristine!" I roared. "You quit messin' around. You come out here, right now! You hear me?"

Still nothing.

I walked down the hall to Mama and Daddy's bedroom and searched. She wasn't there. Or in the laundry room, living room, or kitchen.

A sudden chill made the little bumps pop up on my arms as I remembered what she said:

"Out."

The chill bumps scampered across my chest and shoulders.

I raced through the house. The back door was open, but the screen was latched. I pressed my cheek against it and looked out. Kristine wasn't on the swing set. In fact, she was no place in the backyard.

Instantly I spun and raced for the front door.

Kristine wasn't on the porch. Then—then my heart stopped. I saw her.

Kristine was sitting on the edge of the paved road. She had a little mound of gravel between her feet. She was scooping up more gravel with her pudgy little hands and adding it to the pile.

For just a minute I'd taken my eyes off her. I'd gotten busy cleaning my room. Now my baby sister was sitting on the edge of the road.

And—in that same second that I saw her—I heard the sound of a car.

A motor roared. Tires squealed. It was the black Chevy, the one that raced up and down our road.

I leaped from the porch and charged across the yard. The glare of headlights caught the corner of my eye. Tires screamed at the corner by the bridge. The beams of light swept across our yard.

I ran harder. My heart pounded in my ears so much I thought my head was going to burst. The lights, aimed like the sights of a gun, settled on my baby sister. She still sat on the edge of the road. She scooped up another handful of gravel and dribbled it on the pile between her feet.

"KRISTINE!!!"

I screamed her name. I could never reach her in time.

CHAPTER
8

Above the sound of my heart pounding in my ears, I could hear the motor. It roared louder—closer.

The tires squealed again. The headlights swept back across me as the '57 Chevy pulled into our driveway and slid to a stop in the gravel.

Teeth grinding, fists clenched, I raced to Kristine and scooped her up in my arms. With trembling hands, I clutched my baby sister tight against my chest. She screamed and started crying.

I usually hated the sound of Kristine's crying. This time it didn't matter. I had her. She was safe.

My forehead felt damp and clammy. My knees felt weak. I held her tighter.

Kristine cried even louder than before. I guess

she hadn't seen me coming. I guess she felt like something had crept up—come from the evening shadows—and attacked her. I guess I scared her.

I didn't scare her half as much as she scared me! Despite her crying and struggling, I hugged her even tighter. I kissed her smack on top of the head, over and over.

"Don't you ever do that again!" I sniffed. "Don't you ever run off like that!"

Then I remembered the black Chevy in our drive-way. Time and again I'd heard and seen that black Chevy race past our house. I'd heard the motor roar and the tires squeal. I'd seen the back end of the car fishtail as it rounded the curve right before the bridge. That was terrifying enough, but to have Kristine out near the road. To see, in my mind's eye, what might have happened if the car hadn't turned into our driveway and stopped made my blood feel like ice.

"That dumb idiot," I growled above Kristine's crying. "Drives like a fool. He's gonna kill some-body one of these days. I'm gonna . . ."

I tucked Kristine under my arm and marched toward the car. I could see the guy behind the wheel. In the evening shadows I couldn't see his face, but I could see how big he was. I didn't care if he was a grown-up high-school kid. I didn't care if he jumped out of his car and beat the tar out of me. He didn't have the right to come tearing down our road like he always did. He didn't have the right to darn near run over my baby sister.

I was gonna tell him. I was gonna use the same bad words that Daddy did when he yelled out the front screen at the speeding car. It didn't matter what happened to me, I was going to . . .

I wasn't going to do anything.

I hadn't even gotten halfway across the yard when the tires spun. Gravel shot out and sprayed against the porch. The black Chevy shot backward from our driveway and onto the pavement. The motor revved a couple of times, then the tires screamed. In the blink of an eye the car sped off across the bridge and around the corner.

When the dust cleared from all the loose gravel that had been kicked up, Jimmy was standing in our driveway.

"Hey, dude." He waved. "What's cookin'? You and the brat been out for your evenin' walk or somethin'?"

I marched right up to him. I didn't look at him. Instead, I glared after the speeding car.

"Who is that dumb idiot?" I demanded.

Jimmy glanced over his shoulder at where the red taillights disappeared around the corner.

"That ain't no dumb idiot." He gave a little laugh. "That's my cousin. That's Bubba."

Kristine was still crying. I took her from under my arm and cuddled her against me.

"He's a dumb idiot," I repeated. "He needs to learn how to drive."

Jimmy's head tilted way to the side.

"Learn to drive?" he scoffed. "Bubba's one of the best drivers in the whole state of Louisiana. Got one of the best cars, too." Jimmy had a backpack in his left hand. He slung it over his shoulder and started toward the house. With a jerk of his head, he motioned me to follow. "The guys down at Connors were telling how Bubba was over to Shreveport last year and had three cop cars on his tail. He outrun all of 'em. Got clean away. Man, you don't do stuff like that 'less you're a good driver and you got a souped-up car."

I stood for a second and glared at the back of Jimmy's head. "Kristine was out by the road. She snuck out, and I didn't know it. If that idiot hadn't pulled into the driveway . . ."

"Quit callin' Bubba an idiot," Jimmy said over his shoulder. "We seen the kid when we come across the bridge. Even if Bubba hadn't pulled into the drive, he'd a dodged around her. He'd a missed her by a mile. Bubba's cool. He knows what he's doin'. Now, quit griping about it. You shouldn't have been lettin' the kid play out in the road in the first place. Got anything to eat?"

I stood there, shaking from being scared and mad and everything else—all rolled up and mixed up at once. Kristine was still whimpering.

Jimmy opened the front screen and walked into the house like he owned the place. After a moment, Kristine and I followed him.

We put Jimmy's pack on my bed and went to the kitchen. I plopped Kristine in her high chair and strapped her in. Then I fixed Jimmy a tuna sandwich and dumped some chips on a plate for him. He sat at the table and chomped on the sandwich.

"Got anything to drink?" he mumbled through his big mouthful of food.

Kristine was still whimpering. "Yeah," I answered. "Let me get my sister calmed down."

Mama didn't like me giving Kristine Cokes and stuff. She said milk was a lot better for her. I fixed her a Coke anyway. She liked Coke a bunch, and I figured it was a good way to make her forget about the scary time we'd just had and to get her quiet before Mama got home.

After I had her settled, I fixed Jimmy a Coke.

Then I fixed myself a sandwich. When I went to sit down with Jimmy, he held out his empty plate toward me.

"Wasn't bad." He kind of belched. "Fix me another one."

I took the food off my plate and gave it to Jimmy. Then I went back and made another sandwich for me. Jimmy was just about finished with his second sandwich when I finally sat down.

I wasn't very hungry. I took a couple of bites and poured Kristine some more Coke. When I came back Jimmy pushed his chair away from the table. He kind of rocked back and patted his stomach. Then he burped. It was one of those loud, long burps, too.

"I was hungry." He chuckled. "Got any cookies or somethin' for dessert?"

He didn't even wait for me to answer. Instead, he got up and started prowling around in the cabinets. He opened one door after another. Then he looked around in the pantry and finally went through our refrigerator. When he didn't find anything that he wanted, he took off to explore the rest of the house.

I'd never do anything like that at somebody else's house. Well, maybe if we were best friends and spent a bunch of time at each other's houses—then, going through the refrigerator and prowling was okay. But this was the first time Jimmy had ever been to my house. It just didn't seem right.

About three seconds after I heard Mama drive up, Jimmy came scurrying back to the kitchen. Quickly, he grabbed another handful of chips and sat down.

Mama seemed a lot calmer and happier now that her tooth was fixed. I introduced Jimmy to her. She remembered me telling her that he was coming to spend the night.

"Ted told me you were coming over." She smiled. "But I lost a filling out of my tooth and had to make a quick run to the dentist's office. You boys find something to eat?"

"Yes, Mrs. Greene," Jimmy answered politely. "Only we didn't have nothin' for dessert. I got kind of a sweet tooth."

Mama cocked an eyebrow. "I could mix up a batch of cookies, I guess."

Jimmy's eyes sparkled. "You know how to make them chocolate ones with the oatmeal in 'em? Not the ones you stick in the oven, them other kind?"

Mama rubbed her lip, like the feeling was coming back after the shot the dentist gave her.

"The Chocolate No-bake Cookies?"

"Yeah, them's the ones." Jimmy nodded. "You make us some of those?"

Mama wiggled her lip again and smiled.

"Sure. I think we have everything we need."
Then she turned to me and asked: "Have any problems with Kristine while I was gone?"

The bite of tuna sandwich I'd just started to swallow got stuck about halfway down my throat.

CHAPTER
9

I swallowed the tuna. It didn't slide. Instead, it clumped together in one big chunk and slowly worked its way down my throat like the lump a frog makes when it gets swallowed by a snake.

I wanted to tell Mama about Kristine slipping out the front door. I wanted to tell her about the black car and the way the tires squealed, and about Kristine playing at the side of the road. I wanted to tell her that I knew who the guy was who drove the black car. His name was Bubba Larkin and he was a total creep. He was Jimmy's cousin. I wanted to tell her *everything*.

"No trouble at all," I answered.

Mama fixed the cookies in a pan on the stove. Then she took a spoon and scooped them out onto some waxed paper she'd put on the counter. Jimmy gobbled down nearly half of them while they were still so gooey they wouldn't come off the waxed paper.

When Mama picked Kristine up to get her ready for bed, she glanced down at the Coke that floated around in the high-chair tray. She shot me an irritated look, but since we had company, she didn't say anything about me giving my sister a Coke.

Jimmy and I watched TV for a while, then went to my room. When we got in bed, I figured we'd talk awhile. Guys always do that when they spend the night with each other. You tell stories, talk about stuff that happens at school, or talk about neat stuff you've done or places you've been.

Jimmy fell asleep.

I lay there in the dark, looking up at the ceiling. Jimmy Weston was a lot different from any friend I'd ever had. He was pushy, the way he'd prowled through the cabinets and the house and the refrigerator, then asked Mama to fix him cookies. Not only cookies—a certain kind of cookie. On top of that, Bubba Larkin, the idiot who drove the black Chevy, was his cousin. But I guess that really wasn't Jimmy's fault. I mean, you can't help who your relatives are.

Still, if it hadn't been for the Witch of Blackwater

Swamp, I would have probably told Jimmy I was sick and he'd better go on home.

If I hadn't been scared to go out in the swamp by myself, if Jimmy wasn't the only guy in school who told me he'd go with me . . . well, I had the feeling that Jimmy Weston just wasn't the kind of guy I wanted for a best friend.

Jimmy paused by a tall cypress tree to wait for me. I walked faster, dodging around a wet spot where water stood on the trail, and caught up with him.

"How much farther you reckon it is?" He leaned around the tree and scanned the little path we had been following.

I shrugged. "Don't know. How long we been walking?"

Jimmy glanced at his wrist. I hadn't noticed his watch before. It was gold. Nice and new, it caught the light of the noonday sun, making a little dot of light bounce around on the big tree trunk. The band was a little big and the watch had slipped around on his wrist. Jimmy straightened it.

"We only been walking about twenty minutes." He frowned and scratched his nose. "Usually takes me about twenty minutes or so to walk a mile, but the way this river twists and turns and all the trees and stuff we've had to dodge around . . ." He gave a little shrug. "Hard telling how far we've walked. Let's keep going."

I took the lead this time. The river had been in sight, to our right, since we'd started. At first, the little path we followed was made of hard-packed dirt. But the farther we walked, the more the path turned to mud. It was a black mud that stuck to the bottom of my tennis shoes. It was a gooey mess that made my feet feel heavy. The wind didn't blow very hard down in the river bottom either. The heat, the thick heavy air, and my mud-clogged shoes made each step a chore.

Ahead I could see a thick stand of cypress and willow trees. Water glistened on the ground beneath them. As we neared the trees, I sank deeper into the mud. It was almost to the top of my shoes, and I was about to tell Jimmy that I didn't want to go any farther into the swamp. Just then, on our left, I saw a little path winding up the side of a small hill or river terrace. I kept going.

Walking wasn't so bad on the ridge above the river. The trail led through knee-high grass. The trees by the river were below us on the right and a thick, dense pine forest rimmed the grass meadow on the left. Crows called from the forest. Their shrill, crass caws grated on my ears like someone scraping his fingernails on a chalkboard. The ground was dry and firm, but the path was hard to follow. Little trails branched off from the sides and wound off into the trees on the hill or back down toward the river. It was hard to tell which was the main path and which was only a branch. There were a couple of times when we just had to guess. The side paths were not quite as wide as the main one. Other times, the paths were as wide as the main trail, but they disappeared into dense brush or went right under a big log.

It seemed like we walked forever before the trail turned sharply back toward the river. We moved over the edge of a steep hill.

Suddenly, we were there.

Below us was a brown shack. It stood on a small island. Water, black as the old witch herself, circled the little island on three sides. Beyond, there was a wide sea of marsh grass and swamp. The river, nearly a half-mile away, shimmered and glistened on the far side of the swamp.

A movement caught my eye. White hair, wild as the marsh grass, appeared at the side of the cabin. Then I could see a wrinkled, black face and a mud-brown dress that was tattered and torn.

It was the Witch of Blackwater Swamp!

CHAPTER
10

Like two soldiers in an old war movie, Jimmy and I hit the dirt. We practically dove into the tall grass next to the path. For only a second we lay completely still. Then side by side, we crawled army style to the edge of the ridge.

The old witch hadn't seen us. She walked around the edge of the cabin and went to a boxlike thing made of wire and wood. It stood next to a thick clump of bushes. I propped myself on my elbows and raised myself higher so I could see over the grass.

She opened a hinged door and put something inside. Then she closed the door and went back toward her shack.

I bit my bottom lip. The boxlike thing was a cage.

For some weird reason, I remembered the little fairy tale Mama used to read when I was young. Hänsel and Gretel, I think it was called. I remembered the gingerbread house. I bet it was the same brown color as the witch's shack. I bet she had a big oven inside and . . .

I chased the dumb-little-kid thoughts from my head and concentrated on the island.

There were other cages. Three or four rows of wood frames, covered with wire, lined the outside of the cabin. Another row of cages stood near the clump of dark green bushes. Most were empty. A few had something in them, but we were so far away I couldn't tell what.

When the old witch was out of sight, I crouched on my knees so I could see better. I had to find out what was inside those cages.

The whole island wasn't much bigger than my house. The shack that stood in the very center was old and weathered like it had never seen a coat of paint. There were cracks between the boards where the wind could whip through.

Then I noticed that there wasn't any wind. It was eerie. Behind us, when we'd walked to the edge of the ridge, there'd been a breeze. It had been slight, but the air had still moved a little. Here, just over the edge, it was like we had crossed some invisible line. On this side of the line it was as still as death.

I felt uncomfortable. The marsh grass didn't sway. The leaves on the trees didn't wiggle. The surface of the black water below us was as flat and smooth as a fine polished mirror. I lowered myself to the ground so only my eyes peeked above the grass.

Another movement caught my eye. A small animal of some kind darted around the side of the shack. I couldn't tell what it was, but it sort of dragged its hind end. Then, hot on its heels, the old witch appeared.

"Come back!" Her shrill voice pierced the stillness. "Come back or I wring you stupid neck!"

I raised up higher, trying to see the poor creature she was chasing. The animal darted into the deep green thicket. On my hands and knees, I inched forward, stretching my neck to see over the grass.

Suddenly, the soft clump of dirt I was balancing on gave way. I slipped. Fell.

I grabbed at the ground, trying to get my balance. It was no use. I tumbled, headfirst, and started rolling.

Arms flailing and feet churning, I rolled and rolled and rolled. I tumbled and flopped and crashed through the grass. I couldn't stop.

Faster and faster, I spun down the hill. I was headed straight for the black water at the bottom of the steep slope. Out of control, I was headed right for the island—the witch.

Something crunched against my left shoulder. I stopped.

Well, my body stopped. The rest of me kept right on going. I'd rolled so many times coming down the steep hill that my insides kept tumbling and spinning even after my body stopped.

I tried to open my eyes. All they would do was blink. Uncontrollably, they snapped open and shut so quickly that I couldn't get them to stop. My head went round and round and my eyes kept making little circles inside my skull.

Leaning to my right, I tried to sit up. I was so dizzy and off balance, I flopped back. My left arm crunched against whatever it was that stopped my fall.

How long I lay there, trying to make the world quit spinning, I don't know. Finally I was able to force my eyes open. A huge driftwood log lay against my left side. That was what stopped my fall. The log, weathered and baked almost white from the hot Louisiana sun, was what had saved me from landing in the water. I forced myself to focus on it. I stared at it until my eyes stopped rolling.

At last I was able to sit up.

I had landed at the bottom of the steep slope in a

pile of driftwood. I blinked again. I was only ten inches or so from the black water, and the island was less than twenty feet away.

My eyes darted to the thicket beyond the far bank, the place where I had last seen the witch. She wasn't there. Frantically, I looked around for Jimmy. He was no place in sight. Instantly, my eyes returned to the island bank.

Two wooden planks were laid across the water at a narrow gap. Like a bridge, they joined the island to the bank where I lay.

That's where she was.

Dark eyes glared at me. Her evil look pierced through me like a spear. Her hair was as white as the flour Mama used for pancakes. It clumped wild and spindly about her head, like some cloudy, out-of-focus halo. She was old. Deep wrinkles, as deep and wide as the cracks in her wood cabin, furrowed her face. I was so close I could see every one. A gnarled hand came up from her side. A shaking, crooked finger stuck out.

She pointed. She took another step toward the bridge.

I couldn't get up. The driftwood, as crooked and bent as the gnarled finger that was pointing at me, seemed to grab my feet and hold me tight.

The old witch was coming after me!

CHAPTER
11

"STOP!"

Her shrill scream didn't slow me down a bit. Somehow, I managed to kick and struggle to my feet. I charged up the steep hill. My legs churned. I grabbed handfuls of grass to pull myself along. No way was I going to stop. No way was I going to let her get hold of me.

"HELP!"

The word *stop* made me run harder. But when the old witch screamed "Help" . . .

Still clamoring up the steep slope on all fours, I hesitated. I glanced back over my shoulder.

She wasn't coming across the bridge. In fact she'd moved away from the two wooden planks and was standing between the brush thicket and the water.

Frowning, I turned around to look at her.

Her wrinkled, craggy face seemed to soften.

"Help, first. Run away, later."

I straightened, tilting my head to the side. Her gnarled finger pointed at the brush. "Squeaky get in water, dey get him. He be dead. You help chase back in house."

I took a step toward the hill, then stopped.

"What?"

She pointed at the pile of driftwood where I'd landed only moments before. "You jump up and down. Yell. Shout. Throw wood at water and at other end of lime bushes."

Cautiously, I took a step toward her. She nodded and pointed again at the driftwood. "Throw."

The old witch knelt down and looked into the thick, green brush. I picked up a chunk of wood and tossed it. It went "plop" in the still black water. She turned and shot an angry glance in my direction.

"Throw wood and yell!"

I shrugged. Then I started throwing one chunk of wood after another. I waved my arms and jumped up and down and yelled and shouted. Again I threw more driftwood.

The old witch kept crawling around at the edge of the thicket. She peeked under the low-hanging branches. Once in a while, she reached out and shook one of the shrubs.

After a minute or two, I saw something at the side of the brush. It looked like a half-grown opossum. There was white gauze wrapped around his back legs and he dragged himself from the thicket with his front paws.

"There!" I pointed.

Quickly, the old woman scrambled to her feet. She wasn't very fast so it took her a few tries, but she finally caught the opossum before he could slip back into the thick brush. She picked him up tenderly in her wrinkled hands. The little opossum made a squeaking sound and snapped at her. She kind of cradled him against her like I'd seen Mama do with Kristine when she fell down and got hurt or something. The opossum bit at her again. She just held him in her arms and smiled. After a moment, he quit biting and wrapped his ratty tail around her wrist.

"Opossum slow, Squeaky," she told him. Her voice was soft and gentle. "Da opossum with two broke legs be real slow. How you run so fast?"

I could tell by the way she acted that she wasn't trying to hurt the little animal. She cared for it.

I felt kind of proud of myself for helping. When

she turned toward me, a big smile stretched across my cheeks. When she said "Thank you," I was going to nod and tell her "You're welcome."

Her dark eyes studied me a moment.

"Run away, now."

My smile drooped to a frown.

"Huh?"

"You friend run away when you fall down da hill. You run away now, too."

"But . . ." I stammered, "aren't you even going to say . . ."

"Go home!" she snapped, cutting me off. Then she turned and started for her shack.

I put my hands on my hips, glaring after her. As she walked away, my eyes fell on another cage near her. A little squirrel was sitting in it, munching on something.

"Hey?" I called. "What other animals you got? You a vet or something?"

She spun around. Her dark eyes cut into me.

"Animals no like people. I no like 'em, neither. You go home."

Her tone was angry and stern. I took a step backward. Her dark eyes didn't leave me. She shooed me with her free hand. "You go home. Get away from dis place. I *get* you, if you don't!"

She wheeled and marched off to her cabin. I stood

on the bank, pouting, glaring at the back of her white, wispy hair until she disappeared around the corner. When I heard a door slam I turned and stomped up the hill.

"That's all the thanks I get," I muttered as I marched up the slope. "Try to help somebody . . ."

I expected to find Jimmy hiding in the tall grass when I topped the ridge, but he was no place in sight. When I called out his name, he didn't answer. I headed down the path for home.

"Some friend he is," I mumbled to the crows that called from the forest as I passed. "Almost fall into Blackwater Swamp. Almost get caught by the old witch. He doesn't even stick around to see if I'm still alive or not. Some friend. He's probably hiding under my bed at home."

Jimmy hadn't run home. He wasn't hiding under my bed either. He was standing beside the big cypress tree, where the trail came down from the hill and followed the riverbank. He smiled and waved when I rounded the bend.

"Thanks a lot," I growled. "Some friend to run out on me like that."

"I . . . ah . . . ," he stammered. "I thought you was hurt. I didn't run out on ya. I was going for help."

"Yeah, right," I snorted.

He smiled again and gave a big shrug.

"Really, Ted," he lied. "I was gonna go get your dad. I was almost to your house . . . then . . . well, I didn't want to scare your folks if you was all right. So, I come back to check. I just got here and . . ."

Listening to his lame excuses, I couldn't keep my teeth from making a crunching sound as they ground together. I shook my head.

"Come on, Jimmy, let's go home."

CHAPTER
12

We'd been gone a long time. Jimmy's mother, Barbara, picked him up about fifteen minutes after we got back to the house. I was glad he was gone. I was even happier that his idiot cousin, Bubba, didn't come after him. I just knew if that jerk had roared into our driveway in his black Chevy, Daddy would have gone out and beat the tar out of him.

As soon as Jimmy left, I went to tell Mama and Daddy about what happened to Kristine last night. I had to. And as soon as I'd told them what I *had to*, I *wanted to* tell them about the Witch of Blackwater Swamp.

Daddy already knew the guy's name was Bubba Larkin, although he didn't know he was any kin to Jimmy. He knew because last week he'd gone to town and talked to Sheriff Thibodeaux. The sheriff told him the reason the patrolman hadn't caught Bubba for speeding or reckless driving was probably because the patrolman who worked our area was Bubba's cousin. He said now that he knew who we were talking about, he'd assign another patrolman to our neighborhood and see if that person couldn't get the situation under control.

Mama and Daddy weren't too happy about Kristine. They didn't get onto me much for not watching her, like I was supposed to. Mama did say that she thought I was "responsible" enough to look in on her more often, or at least to make sure the front screen was latched. Then she added, "Maybe you're not as grown-up as I'd hoped."

Like I said, they didn't chew on me much. After the little lecture was over, I started telling about the old witch and all the cages and animals—I *loved* animals.

Mama didn't listen for long, because Kristine woke up from her nap and started whimpering. Daddy listened up until I got to the part where she caught the opossum and told me to go home instead of thanking me.

"I want to sneak back out and see what other kind of animals she's got in those cages. You think I . . ."

Daddy got up from the table.

"I got to get that darned lawn mowed before it gets dark," he announced. Then, over his shoulder he added, "Can't believe the grass starts growing so early in these parts. And you quit messin' around out in that swamp. The old woman doesn't want people around her place. You do like she says."

When Mama came back, I wanted to tell her the part of the story she'd missed. I wanted to ask her if she really thought the old woman was a witch and if she thought it was okay for me to sneak back out there and see what she was up to.

I never got the chance. Mama shoved Kristine at me and went to the refrigerator.

"You can tell me your story later, dear. I need to get supper started. Watch Kristine."

WATCH KRISTINE! That was the story of my life!

Don called Sunday after church. He told me that his dad got him a new bicycle. We met at Parsons' Grocery and rode to the park. Don brought a loaf of bread to feed the ducks. We didn't chase them— well, not much. At least, we didn't try to run over them on our bikes. We rode after them just a little, then parked our bicycles and tossed pieces of bread to them. When we emptied the bread sack that Don brought, we rode down the back of the dam and climbed over the fence. We had a lot of fun exploring the little creek.

Don found a wide shady place in the stream that he figured would be a great spot to go fishing. He told me that the next time we came, he'd bring his fishing rod and an extra one for me. When we left, he asked if I would loan him my autographed copy of *Scared Stiff* for his next book report. I promised I'd bring it Monday morning.

My copy of *Scared Stiff* wasn't on my dresser. It had vanished and I couldn't find it anyplace. I remembered Don looking at the book when he came over to spend the night. I remembered picking it up and thinking about reading it for my next book report, then putting it down and finding *Weasel*. It wasn't as long, and I figured I could get through it more quickly. But for the life of me, I couldn't remember where I'd left that autographed book. I could have sworn it was on my dresser, but . . .

First thing Monday morning, I was going to find Don and tell him he'd have to get another book, at least until I figured out what I'd done with the one he wanted.

I never got around to telling him, not until we

were in the lunchroom on Monday. The reason neither one of us even thought about it until then was because of all the excitement.

When I got off the bus, I noticed two police cars and a sheriff's car parked in front of the school. Seeing a cop car at school wasn't all that unusual. Policemen sometimes came and talked to us about safety or drugs. Seeing three police cars *was* unusual, though.

The kids waiting outside for the bell to ring didn't seem to have any idea what was going on. Coach Reicher was usually outside with us. He yelled at people if they got to running too much or scuffling. But even Coach wasn't around this morning.

When the bell finally rang, we bumped and crunched and kind of climbed over each other to get inside. There were a couple of men in blue uniforms talking with Mrs. Burton, our principal. They stood around in front of the office and pointed down the hall. Then they scratched their heads and pointed in the other direction.

Jimmy met me at homeroom. I'd never seen him act so excited.

"What's going on?" he asked. "What're all the cops doin' here?"

I shrugged.

Mrs. Whitbeck came in about the time we got to our desks. All the girls rushed over to ask what had happened. She made everybody sit down.

"The school had a break-in over the weekend," she announced.

"What'd they steal?" Jimmy called out from the desk next to mine.

Mrs. Whitbeck put her grade book on her desk and shook her head.

"They don't know what all is missing, yet. We do know they stole some picture money from the office. They took the copy machine and some computers from the math department."

"Copy machine?" Barry Talder asked, almost laughing. "That mean we don't have to do no more work sheets?"

Everybody kind of giggled. Mrs. Whitbeck cocked an eyebrow.

"Don't worry about it, Barry. I'll make a special point to see that you have plenty of work to do."

We all shut up.

It was exciting. But like usual, things quieted down as soon as school started. Everything was back to normal until we went to fourth hour.

My fourth-hour class was physical education. I liked it and I liked Coach Reicher. Only today, Coach wasn't in a very good mood.

Our class came into the gym and sat down in rows on the floor. Coach called them "squads," instead of rows, but it was all the same. He usually told us what game we were going to play, and we chose teams. Or he told us what kind of activities we were going to work on, and we went to line up by the balance beam or the climbing rope or whatever.

Today, we got a lecture.

Seemed like whoever broke into the school over the weekend didn't only steal money out of the office and take some of the computers and the copy machine, they also stole most of our PE stuff. Balls, bats, footballs, basketballs—all the fun stuff was gone.

"We'll just have to make do," Coach Reicher told us. "Why anyone would steal computers *and* footballs is beyond me. You can't sell footballs. They've got the words Property of Lakeview Athletic Department stamped into the side of them with big letters, so there's no way someone could sell them. Why anyone would steal them, I don't know, but someone did. So we won't be able to play many sports the rest of this school year."

"Did they get the dodgeballs, too?" someone called, cutting him off.

"I'm afraid so." Coach sighed.

Everybody moaned at the same time. Dodgeball was our favorite game!

"You reckon it was some kid?" Gary Marland asked.

Coach shook his head. "No, a kid wouldn't steal the computers or know where money was hidden in the office. I figure it was a 'real' robber, instead of kids." He paused and scratched his chin. "Still, why our footballs and . . ."

"Can't we get new balls?" Doug Boswell asked.

Coach nodded. "The school insurance will pay to replace things, but we won't be able to get what we need right away. It usually takes a few months for the insurance money to come in. Then we have to fill out the order forms, and we have to wait for the company to deliver." He shrugged. "We're probably talking next school year before we can get everything replaced." He cleared his throat and stuffed his hands in the pockets of his shorts. "That's why I want to speak to you today about stealing. Stealing is wrong. When you steal something, when you take something that belongs to someone else . . ."

Everybody kind of slumped. Jimmy laced his fingers behind his head and stretched out on the floor. I leaned on one elbow.

"You see," Coach Reicher continued, "when

someone steals something, it affects a lot of people.
It's not just money or things. Just think of all the fun
and activities we're going to miss because some
sneaking thief . . ."

His lecture about the evils of stealing lasted the
whole period.

I ate with Don at lunch. Jimmy came in and sat
with us. Don didn't act like he cared much for
Jimmy. The way Jimmy had acted when he spent
the night with me, I wasn't that crazy about him
either. We let him sit with us, though.

Don asked if I wanted to ride bikes to the park
again. Jimmy wanted to go, too.

I stabbed my fork into my tater-tot so hard, it
went clear through and made a crunching sound
when it poked into the Styrofoam tray.

"I can't," I muttered, "I got to WATCH KRIS-
TINE!"

CHAPTER
13

The note I found on the TV when I got home after school was the first bright spot in an otherwise horrible day.

> Ted,
> Took Kristine shopping with me. You can go play. Be careful and be home before dark.
>
> > Love,
> > Mama

I threw my backpack on the bed and ran straight for the phone. I called Don, and his mom told me that he'd gone to ride his bike with a friend. No one answered at Jimmy's house. Quickly, I took my school clothes off and dumped them on the floor. I kicked my shoes into the closet and found my old tennies and my dirty jeans. If I hurried, maybe I could catch them at Parsons' or at the park.

I laced my tennis shoes and took off for the door. Suddenly, something grabbed my foot. I tripped and landed, spread-eagle, smack in the middle of my room.

Irritated, I jumped up and looked down at what had tripped me. It was the blue sweatshirt I'd worn Friday. That and a bunch of other stuff were dumped all over my floor.

Mama's gonna be chewing on me for sure, I thought. It'll only take a second to clean up.

I grabbed stuff and trotted down to the laundry. On the way back, I glanced into Mama and Daddy's room. About two steps beyond the open door, I stopped. I backed up and looked again.

Daddy's big black binoculars were sitting on his dresser. I stood in the open doorway and looked at them. A sly smile tugged at the corners of my mouth. Biking with Don could wait.

With my bottom resting on my heels, I sat up above the tall grass and turned the focus wheel on the binoculars. The top of the ridge was a long ways from the witch's shack. Daddy's binoculars were good binoculars, though. It made me feel like I was right down there on the island.

The old witch was no place in sight.

Near the door of her shack I could see a huge black pot. I hadn't seen it the last time I was here. When I looked at it and remembered the stories about her casting her evil spells, my insides felt cold. The pot was nearly as big around as I was tall. There were ashes beneath it. The thing was supported above the ground by a steel rod suspended between two forked logs.

The little squirrel I'd seen was still in the cage. I studied him a moment. There weren't any bandages or stuff on him like I'd seen on the opossum. The cage next to him was empty, but next to that one I could see some baby rabbits. They were the brown ones, the wild kind. They were so tiny, they barely had their eyes open. The cage next to that . . .

I didn't see the cage next to that.

There was an old shoe instead, with a hole in the side of it. A black, crooked, little toe stuck out the hole. I followed a black leg up to the hem of a tattered, wrinkled dress. Then past old gnarled hands up to a wrinkled angry face.

The Witch of Blackwater Swamp stood beside the cage of baby rabbits. She wasn't looking at them.

Her eyes were focused straight on me. How she'd seen me, way up here on top of the ridge, I had no idea. But she had.

I took the binoculars from my eyes and looked down at her. She shooed me with her hand.

"You go away. You go home!"

I held the binoculars at my side and stood up.

"All I want to do is watch the animals," I called to her.

"Git!"

"How come you got to be so cranky? I'm just . . ."

"Go home!"

"No!"

I put the binoculars back to my eyes and stared at her. She stared at me. We both stood there for a long time. Finally, she put a bowl on top of the rabbit cage. She started toward the bridge.

"You go home or I get you."

I held my ground. The old woman started across the boards.

"I gonna come up dis hill and get you," she threatened.

I wanted to run, but I didn't. I took the binoculars from my face and stood there. She started up the path, but when I didn't run, she finally stopped.

There was a totally disgusted look on her face. She glared at me, then with a snort, turned and walked back across the bridge.

I sat down in the middle of the path so I wouldn't have to fight the tall grass. I focused the binoculars on her once more. She opened the cage and took out one of the baby rabbits. Then holding it in one hand, she reached into the bowl she'd set on top of the cage. She took an eyedropper and squeezed some milk from the bowl into the baby rabbit's mouth. She did that about three times, then put the rabbit back in the cage and got another one.

"You're feeding them?" I called, putting the binoculars in my lap. "They lose their mama or something?"

She didn't answer. She didn't even turn to look at me.

When she finished with the rabbits, she went around the corner of her shack. After a time she came back into view. In one hand she carried a big tin bucket, in the other, a hatchet. It had a wood handle. My hands shook so hard, I didn't even think about picking up the binoculars again.

The old woman skirted the far side of the green thicket and came to the edge of the water. She set the bucket in the water and pounded on the side with the blunt end of the hatchet. Then she reached into the bucket and threw something into the black water.

"What ya doin' now?" I called out.

Again she ignored me. She didn't even glance up. She pitched another handful of stuff from the bucket into the water. I scanned the mirror-smooth surface of the black swamp.

Suddenly a head appeared. It was small and round. Next to it, another and another. The binoculars felt cold when I put the eyepiece underneath my nose and peered over the top.

Little heads were popping up all over the water. I looked through the binoculars again, but I still couldn't tell what they were. Snakes, turtles, frogs—I was too far away, even with the binoculars.

I was just about to get to my feet and sneak a little closer, when the heads began to disappear. One at a time, they sucked under the water with little jerks that left round ripples on the smooth surface.

In a matter of seconds, I could see nothing on the water except the reflection of the white puffy clouds that floated across the sky.

Then . . .

Another head appeared. This one wasn't like the others. The head I saw now was *huge!*

It was as big around as both my father's fists stuck together. At first I thought it must be an alligator or a crocodile or something.

Quickly, I snatched the binoculars back to my eyes. I jammed them against my face so hard, I almost poked my eyes out. Blinking, I took the binoculars down and rubbed my sore eyelids. Then more carefully, I brought them back to look again.

There were two heads now. Then a third broke the mirrorlike surface.

Like the others, the heads were round. I focused my binoculars on the largest one. At the front of the head I could see nostrils. A beaklike thing hung down over a mouth. It was a sharp point that covered the bottom jaw.

"It's a turtle," I whispered.

Then his shell broke the surface of the black swamp. A sharp spiny ridge, like a tiny mountain range, ran down the middle of the shell. Two other smaller ridges were on either side. The turtle was as long as I was from my neck to my bottom. Dark and mossy, the mountainous body followed the head toward the old witch.

I jumped to my feet as quick as Mrs. Dobie did that day Jimmy stuck the tack in her chair at school.

"It's a turtle," I called out. "I've never seen a turtle that big." I took a couple of steps down the path, trying to get closer. "I didn't know turtles got that big. Well, not except for sea turtles. What are those?"

The old woman dumped the rest of the bucket into the water. Then she turned and went back to her cabin. I watched as the huge turtles gobbled up whatever it was she'd thrown to them. After a while their massive heads and shells slipped back into the deep. In a few seconds, the little heads started to appear again. The smaller turtles swam in to scavenge up what was left.

I'd only watched them a moment when I noticed the darkness. Shadows stretched from the forest behind me, clear to where I stood. Long, tall, dark shadows that told of evening and night.

With a jerk I spun around and looked to the west. The sun was already down behind the trees. I didn't know I'd stayed so long. I'd have to run if I was going to make it home before dark.

CHAPTER
14

Headlights shined on the branches of the trees near the river. It was Mama, pulling into the driveway. I knew she'd see me if I followed the trail to the bridge, so I left the path and cut across our backyard. I could hear her talking to Kristine at the front door as I opened and slipped in the back.

Quick as a cat, I raced down the hall, put Daddy's binoculars back on the dresser and dove into my room.

"Ted?" Mama called, appearing at my doorway.

"Hi, Mama." I smiled and held my breath so she wouldn't hear me panting. "You have a good time shopping?"

She smiled back. "Yeah. Come and play with Kristine a minute while I put things away."

As soon as she turned her back, I gulped down a huge breath of air.

"Your dad called," she said as I followed her down the hallway. "He gets to come home early tonight. If you'll get Kristine in her high chair and keep her busy, I'll try to put things away and have supper ready when he comes in."

I fixed Kristine some milk in her cup. Then I got some of her little toy men and put them on her tray. She didn't want to play with them. She just stuck them in her mouth and got milk and spit all over the plastic. When she did play, it was the "Me throw, You pick up" game.

Kristine dropped one of the little toys on the floor and pointed.

"Mine."

As soon as I picked it up for her, she threw another one off the other side of her tray. It seemed like the game went on forever—well, at least until Daddy got home and we all sat down for supper. After we finished eating, I asked Daddy if I could borrow his binoculars. I didn't like taking them without his permission. At the same time, I couldn't tell him why I wanted them because he'd told me to stay away from the swamp and from the old witch's shack.

"Sure," Daddy said. Then he hesitated a moment and sort of looked at me out of the corner of one eye. "What do you need 'em for? Got some cute little neighbor girl you're trying to keep an eye on?"

"Daddy!" I whined.

He wiggled his eyebrows up and down and gave a little chuckle.

"Well?"

I crinkled my nose and shook my head. "I don't even like girls, Daddy. I saw this turtle down on the river. All I saw was his head and part of his shell, but the thing was *huge!* I want to see if I can spot him again."

He frowned.

"How huge is *huge?*"

I reached over and folded his fingers into fists. Then holding his wrists, I put his hands together.

Daddy had big hands. As I looked down at his fists I realized that even both together weren't as big as the turtle's head.

"Just his head was bigger than your two fists," I told him.

Wrinkles etched his forehead.

"That big, huh?"

I nodded.

Daddy stroked his chin. "We're too far inland for a leatherback or a loggerhead." He tilted his head to the side. "It didn't have a spiny ridge down its back, did it? Or a real long tail?"

"I couldn't see its tail, but it did have a ridge down its back. In fact there was a real tall ridge in the center and two kind of shorter ones on either side."

Daddy's eyes flashed. "My gosh," he gasped. Then he leaped to his feet and almost knocked his chair over when he trotted to the living room. I followed him and watched as he dug through the bookcase beside the TV. When he didn't find what he wanted, he dropped to his knees and dug around in the cabinet. Finally, he made a groaning sound when he got to his feet. He had a small book in his hand. It was white with little pictures of snakes and lizards and turtles on the front.

I went back to the kitchen with him and sat watching while he thumbed through the book. At last he found what he wanted. He bent the book open, wide, and turned it toward me.

"Did it look like this?" he asked, pointing at a picture.

"It was mostly under the water." I shrugged. "I can't tell."

He reached over and covered up the bottom part of the picture with his hand. "Just the head and the back, then. The sharp-pointed, jagged beak? The peaks or ridges down the back of the shell? Did it look like that?"

I smiled. With Daddy's hand covering the bottom part of the picture, what was left looked exactly like what I'd seen at the witch's shack.

"That's it!" I said. "There was moss and crud on the shell, but that's it."

Daddy slumped back in his chair and left me holding the book. "I can't believe it." He sighed. "That's an alligator snapper. Those things were on the endangered species list when I was your age."

I glanced down at the book, then back at Daddy.

"What does that mean? That list thing?"

"Endangered species list?"

"Yeah."

Daddy rubbed a finger across his eyebrow. "Well, when an animal is hunted almost to extinction or when its habitat is destroyed and it can't find food and can't reproduce, the government puts it on a special list. It means that the animal is in trouble. It means that if we're not careful, we could lose that kind of animal forever." He looked up at the ceiling and smiled. "I haven't heard of an alligator snapper for years. Alligators and the giant whooping crane were on the list, too. There was a lot of press and stuff on TV about the efforts to restore those two species. There were even articles about how the alligator has done so well that it's causing problems in the more populated areas in Florida. Nobody ever mentioned the snappers. You know, those things can get up to a hundred and fifty pounds? Shoot, over a hundred and fifty. They're big enough to snap a man's leg off if they ever got hold of him. I figured they were all gone."

Daddy liked animals. But I'd never seen him so excited about something, not since he'd found out Mama was going to have Kristine, anyway.

When he quit looking up at the ceiling and turned back to me, he seemed a bit suspicious.

"You sure that's what you saw? I mean, was it really that big?"

I nodded.

"That's what I saw."

"You sure?"

"I'm sure."

"Where did you see him?"

My head jerked so hard, the muscles in the back of my neck felt like somebody stabbed me with a knife.

That was the one question I didn't think Daddy would ask. The one question I hoped—no, prayed—that he wouldn't.

I swallowed the lump that stuck in my throat. I tried to smile.

CHAPTER
15

I felt kind of sorry for Daddy. He had three days off work. I didn't feel sorry for him because of that. But every morning, as I was leaving for school, he got his binoculars and headed for the river. Every afternoon, when I got home from school, I found him standing by the river looking through them.

I felt totally rotten about the whole thing.

I hadn't really lied to him. I told him I saw the turtle in the river. And . . . well . . . Blackwater Swamp was part of the river—sort of. When he asked me where in the river, I told him "a ways down from the bridge." And the old witch's house *was* "a ways down from the bridge." It was a *long* ways down from the bridge. Still, I hadn't really told him a lie. Well . . . maybe a little lie.

Anyway, I felt like a rotten jerk.

Thursday night Daddy brought his binoculars to my bedroom. "Got to get back to the rig early tomorrow morning. Probably won't get home again until Monday or Tuesday." He tossed the binoculars to me. "You get the chance, see if you can spot that turtle." Then, he tossed a black case on my bed. "Get a picture of it if you can."

I opened the black case. It was Daddy's good camera. I couldn't believe he'd trust me with it. That camera was more important to him than me and Kristine. I mean, when we went on vacation, he wouldn't even let Mama take pictures with the thing.

Him trusting me with his camera made me feel even guiltier.

I never took the camera to Blackwater Swamp. I was scared I might drop it or lose it. I figured it was best to just tell Daddy that I hadn't seen the turtle again.

I went out to the swamp every chance I got. Most times, Mama and Kristine were home when I came in from school. Once in a while, I found a note on the TV that said, "Gone shopping," or "Went for groceries," or "Took Kristine to doctor."

After about three weeks, I didn't even slow down enough to read the notes. If I saw one taped to the TV, I'd grab my old clothes and the binoculars and race to the swamp.

During that time the old witch quit yelling at me. The crows never did, though. Each time I passed the forest, they'd caw and yell. It always sounded like they were scolding me or saying something nasty about me invading their territory.

Each trip to Blackwater Swamp, I caught myself sneaking a little closer to the island. The last time, I stood by the pile of driftwood right across the black water lagoon from the old woman's shack. She never screeched at me "Go home," and never threatened that she was "Gonna get me," if I didn't leave. She just ignored me.

It was more like she tolerated me. She didn't want me there, but I guess she figured it was more trouble to try and run me off.

The little island with the cages was the most fascinating place in the whole world. The old witch was kind of interesting, too.

One day, when I didn't get to go to the swamp, I was playing catch with Don in the front yard. Suddenly, I saw the old woman on the path down by the bridge. She had a big canvas bag over her shoulder.

I watched her until she disappeared into the trees.

The next day, Mama had to get Kristine a booster shot at the clinic. When I got to the driftwood pile, I saw the witch digging around in the canvas bag. She dug out old food scraps and put them in the bucket that she used to feed the turtles. Then she dug out some plastic bags and some white gauze. She washed those in the water and hung them to dry on the thicket. Next, she pulled out an almost empty bottle of alcohol and went inside her cabin. She came back with another bottle and poured the alcohol into that.

The stories about her scavenging in the trash cans around town all made sense now. Only she wasn't a "street woman" hunting for food, or a witch "finding things to cast her evil spells with." She was just an old woman who loved animals. She got food and supplies to take care of them the best way she could.

All sorts of animals came and went. Some, she just put in the cages and fed. Others, the ones that were injured, she took into her shack. A few days later, when I came to watch, she either had them outside in the cages or I never saw them again.

On one of my trips out there, she was taking the bandages off the little opossum I'd helped her catch. For some reason I remembered the day I'd seen her on the bridge and almost killed myself on my bicycle. I remembered the little drops of blood I'd noticed where she had knelt.

"You find Squeaky on the bridge that day?" I called.

She didn't answer.

"He got hit by a car or something, right? You found him and fixed him up?"

She nodded, then put the opossum in one of her cages and went back in her shack.

It was the middle of May before she ever spoke to me. That was the day she let the second litter of baby rabbits go. I was standing by the pile of driftwood when she brought the four rabbits across the wood planks. She'd never come across the bridge when I was there—except for that day she tried to run me off. For a second, I thought about running up the path, only I didn't.

"Don't move," was all she said to me. Then she knelt down and opened the latch on the little cage. "You move, maybe scare da babies. Maybe da turtles get 'em ifn dey get too near da water. Be still!"

Holding my breath and not so much as blinking, I watched the baby rabbits scurry off into the tall grass. And for the first time, I saw the Witch of Blackwater Swamp smile.

* * *

When I wasn't watching her and the animals, I played after school with Don. We rode our bicycles or practiced catch with our baseball and gloves. Jimmy joined us a couple of times, but he usually had things to do after school.

Once we did go over to Jimmy's house to play. On the way there we stopped at Connors. Connors was kind of a gas station, convenience store, and beer joint, all mixed into one.

When we rode our bikes up I saw the black Chevy. Three guys sat on the front of a beat-up-looking Ford pickup parked next to it.

Jimmy wheeled up and stopped in front of them.

"Hey, Bubba. What's doin'?"

A guy who sat between the other two shot him a disgusted look. "Beat it, punk," he growled, "we're busy."

"I want you to meet my friends," Jimmy said cheerfully.

"Get lost!"

The guy was ugly. He had a mean face. His hair was kind of greasy, like he hadn't washed it in a couple of months. He had on a white T-shirt. I could see a pack of cigarettes rolled under one short sleeve. He had a tattoo on his arm. When he raised the cigarette to his lips, I saw a picture of a devil with horns. There was a dagger stuck through the devil's head, and red ink dripped down like blood coming from the blue devil.

Jimmy started to get off his bike, but the guy flipped his cigarette at him. Red ashes flew when it hit his shirt. Jimmy brushed off his shirt and stepped on the smoldering butt by his foot. Then he turned to us.

"I'll go get us a candy bar," he said. "You guys wait here."

Don and I didn't wait there. We moved away and waited on our bicycles for Jimmy to come back. The guys on the truck cursed and laughed, real crude-like, when one of them told a joke or said something dirty.

A black woman in a blue Oldsmobile drove past the corner. They yelled some vulgar stuff at her and called her names. Then they laughed and laughed.

Don and I agreed that we'd never come back to Connors again. We were sure glad when Jimmy finally joined us and got on his bike so we could get out of there.

Jimmy's home wasn't very nice. It smelled of smoke and beer and his mom didn't keep it clean like my mom did. There were dirty dishes in the

sink and on the table. There were ashtrays over-
flowing with cigarette butts and ashes in the living
room. I knew Jimmy and his mom didn't have much
money. Still, she could surely sweep and clean up.
I mean, it didn't take a lot of money to do that.

When we got outside, I found that I'd forgotten to
bring my ball glove. Jimmy said he had an extra one
in the garage with his bat and ball. I started to go
with him to get it, but he told me to go back with
Don.

"Mom don't like nobody messin' around in the
garage but me!"

"I won't go in," I said. "I can wait at the door and
help you carry stuff."

His lips seemed to wrap around his teeth, and he
bit down on them. "I'll get it!" he insisted.

It didn't seem fair. I mean, the night Jimmy spent
with me he went through every room in my whole
house. Now, he wouldn't even let me stand at the
door of the garage while he got a ball glove.

I kind of stuck my nose up at him and went back
to wait with Don.

The last week in May, Daddy got to stay home.
We spent all Saturday walking up and down the
river with the binoculars and the camera. I sure

wanted to tell him where the turtles were, but I just couldn't. I knew he'd wring my neck if he found out that he'd spent all this time on the river for nothing.

The following Saturday, I woke up and found a note on the TV. Mama had a hair appointment, and she'd taken Kristine with her. I dressed and took off for Blackwater Swamp. And . . .

Almost got myself killed.

CHAPTER
16

I usually slept late on Saturdays. How long I'd slept after Mama and Kristine left, I had no idea. I did know that if I was going to get to the swamp and back before Mama got suspicious 'cause I was gone so long, I best get moving.

After I dressed, I grabbed a banana and an apple. I ate them as I walked down the path next to the river. When I finished my snack, I started jogging. I'd been down this path so many times, I felt like I knew every inch of it.

Just before I left the river to climb the hill next to the forest, a strange sound came to my ears. I froze in midstride. My tennis shoe dug into the soft mud. But I didn't wiggle. I didn't even breathe. The sound came again. It was like a bell, only deeper. I frowned.

There were bells on the Catholic church back in Oklahoma. They rang at noon. This bell didn't sound like one of those at all. It was so deep it seemed to rumble instead of ring. In fact, the sound was more like a gong, like one of the big gongs the islanders hit with clubs. I'd seen a few movies on black-and-white, late-night TV when Mama and Dad went dancing and stayed out late. I smiled, remembering those corny old movies.

The sound came again, and a frown tugged at the corners of my mouth. It was a strange, eerie sound, and I couldn't help wonder what could make such a noise here in Louisiana.

The closer I got to Blackwater Swamp, the louder and clearer the noise grew. By the time I topped the ridge above the old woman's shack, I wasn't jogging, I was running.

I kind of gave a little skip-hop as I topped the very peak of the ridge, then charged down the path as fast as I could.

Just as I came over the top, I saw this big, hairy, black lump in front of me.

I was really truckin'. There was no way I could stop. There wasn't even time to dodge to the side and go around it. I put my hands out to cushion the impact. My fingers sunk into coarse black hair. The last thing I saw before I slammed into the thing was a short, black, stumpy tail.

"A bear!" I heard someone scream, not even realizing it was me.

It was like running into a fuzzy brick wall. There was no give to it whatsoever. A startled "WHOOMPF" sound came to my ears. I think the bear stood up, spun around, and tried to swat or bite me—only I don't know for sure.

The reason I wasn't sure what happened next was that when I crashed into the bear, I bounced off. I felt myself flying through the air. I spun around a couple of times, like a ballet dancer doing one of those pirouettes. Then I made kind of a somersault in midair and landed on my bottom in the tall grass beside the path.

I hit with such a jolt it felt like my bottom was trying to go through the top of my head. Only I didn't sit there long.

Not six feet away, the bear glared at me with big dark brown eyes. I could see his white fangs and the slobber that dripped from the corner of one lip.

"WHOOMPF!" he said.

I don't remember getting to my feet. I don't re-

member thinking that I'd run into the back end of a
bear. I don't remember thinking that he was gonna
eat me. I don't remember anything.

The next thing I knew, I was on the path rac-
ing down the hill toward the island, running for
my life.

The path was crooked. The trail was steep. If I
took my eyes from the ground for a split second, I
might trip. I glanced back over my shoulder anyway. The bear was on all fours. His eyes were on
me. He was running down the hill after me!

I ran harder.

"Help!" I screamed at the top of my lungs.
"HELP!"

My left foot slipped a bit when I turned at the pile
of driftwood. I kept my balance and raced for the
little wooden bridge. Frantically, I glanced back.
The bear was still coming down the hill. I might be
able to make the bridge. I might be able to get
across and get to the safety of the old woman's shack.
I might . . .

"Right board!" A shrill piercing scream came to
my ears. "Right side. Right board!"

The witch shouted at me from the side of her
shack. It didn't make sense. I kept running.

"Bear!" I screamed. "Help me!"

I charged across the bridge. My right foot hit

solid wood. When my left came down, there was a little "crack" sound and the board gave some. My right hit solid again. But when my left foot came down a second time, there was a loud popping sound. The thick heavy plank gave beneath my foot. I went flying off the side.

A bone-jarring crash knocked the breath from my chest. I lay flat on my face, gasping for air. I'd been running so hard, the fall had carried me clear across the lagoon. I landed on my chest and stomach on the bank of the island.

Well, most of me landed there.

When I felt the wet about my legs and feet, my eyes almost jumped out of my head. I was partly in the water! That's when I remembered the huge turtles and the bear that was chasing me.

Not even taking time to breathe, I crawled up the bank. My mouth was full of sand, and I couldn't see out of my left eye. It was full of sand, too.

I got up and ran.

I ran smack into the thick green brush.

And suddenly . . .

I wasn't running anymore. The brush wrapped about me like Mama's arms wrapped about Kristine. Only, the limbs weren't tender and caring. They were coarse and hard and unyielding.

Something stung me. It was a sharp, stabbing

pain that made me yell out. Then another sting and another.

At first I thought I'd hit a wasp nest. But when I tried to reach and knock it away, something grabbed my arm. A sharp pain jabbed at my palm and made my hand double into a tight fist. Eyes wide, I looked down.

A long, needle-sharp, green thorn was hooked under the skin near my thumb. As I pulled back it lifted the skin and held me. Gently, I moved my hand the other way. The thorn came out, and I saw a little drop of blood. I tried to run again.

I couldn't move. It hurt.

There were more long, sharp thorns. They were everywhere in the thicket. Each branch was covered with them. Some were nearly three inches long. Broad at the base, they stuck out from the branches into points as sharp as an ice pick.

I was stuck. I couldn't get away. I couldn't move.

In a panic, I looked around for the bear. He was at the bridge.

On the far side of the bank he stopped to sniff at the broken board. Then—slowly—he stepped on the other one and started across.

I jumped and yanked. The thorns dug through my jeans and bit my legs. They held my arms. I couldn't breathe without being jabbed in the stomach or chest. The bear was coming, and I couldn't even run.

Suddenly, the old witch was there. She stood right beside me. Her tight black eyes glared at me.

"STOP!"

I tried to jerk. I tried to rip myself free from the sharp thorns and twisted limbs.

From the corner of my eye, I saw her gnarled black hand. She raised it and brought it down. She bopped me right on top of the head.

My eyes blinked. My head bounced. It took a second for my eyes to focus on her.

"You stop!" Her voice was stern, angry. I started to move again, but she raised her fist over my head.

I stopped. When I did, her angry look softened.

"Da bear come. You do not move. You not try run away. You no wiggle. You stand. No matter what, you not move."

I blinked and gave a tiny nod. Behind her I could see the bear. He stepped from the wood plank and walked straight for us. She turned from me to face him.

I don't know what she said. She used some kind of foreign language that I'd never heard before. Her strange words blended together almost like a chant or something.

The bear looked at me, then at her. He made that

"Whoompf" sound again and reared up on his hind legs. After standing there a moment, kind of teetering and balancing himself, he dropped down on all fours and came toward us.

Her voice was soft, almost a whisper.

"You no move. Da bear maybe sniff you. Maybe lick you. He maybe even put you arm in his mouth. You NO MOVE! Even if you hurt, you no move!"

Then . . .

She turned and walked away.

She left me there. The bear was so close I could see his shiny black nose. I could feel his breath on the back of my hand.

My lips were clamped tight around my teeth. Even with my mouth shut, a little "squeak" came from my throat when his tongue stretched out to touch my bare arm. His tongue was as coarse and rough as driveway gravel.

I *knew* I was going to die.

And . . . the Witch of Blackwater Swamp simply walked off and left me for the bear.

CHAPTER
17

The bear sniffed my hand. Then he licked my arm again with that rough tongue.

He opened his mouth. I could see his long sharp white teeth. I could feel his breath as those huge jaws moved closer to my flesh.

Despite my closed mouth, that little squeaking sound snuck out again. But there was another sound. The sound of a bell—a deep, rumbling bell. A gong.

I remembered the old woman's words. I looked toward the sound, but without moving my head. Only my eyes moved.

The old woman stood near the front of her shack. She leaned over the huge black pot. The wood-handled hatchet was in her hand. She banged the blunt end of it time and again into the side of her big black kettle. The ringing sound that came from it was so deep and loud, it seemed to rattle the bushes.

Just as those powerful jaws were about to close around my wrist, the bear stopped. He raised his head and looked toward the old woman. She said something in the strange language she sometimes used and hit the pot one last time.

The bear crashed through the thorn thicket beside me and lumbered toward the old woman. The long sharp thorns didn't bother him a bit. The old woman dropped the hatchet. She scooted a pan toward the bear with her foot and stepped away. The bear sniffed at whatever was inside, then sat on his haunches and started gobbling it down.

The witch came back to where I was trapped in the thorns.

"Dumb kid," she muttered. One thorn at a time, she helped me get loose. "If bear no get you, lime bush eat you up for sure."

It took forever to pick and pry me loose from the bush. The old woman kept one eye on the bear, talking all the time she worked.

"Lime bush like dry place. Swamp not dry. I plant these, here in sand, because sand not hold water. It dry and lime bush like dry. Birds and animals like lime bush. Feel safe. Good place to hide. Lime bush no like people, though."

She pulled a thorn from my knee.

I winced, but never took my eyes from her or the bear, either one.

"Is he your pet?" I asked.

"Bear no pet. I find when him little. Somebody shoot da mama. I feed and take care. He no pet, though. Just come back, sometime, to say 'Hi' and see if I feed him."

"Is he gentle?"

"No. Da bear, he eat your face off."

"But he's a black bear. I thought they were supposed to be gentle. I mean—I know grizzlies aren't gentle, but . . ."

"Wild bear! Dey stay away from people unless da peoples bother dem."

"I didn't know there were any bears in Louisiana."

"Not many," she said. "Lots in swamp, when I was young woman. Not many now." She frowned and unhooked a thorn from my shirt. "Why you try and run over da bear for?"

I almost laughed.

"I didn't try to run over him. I was running to see what was making that 'gong' sound, and so I'd have more time to watch you and the animals. I came over the top of the hill and there he was. I couldn't . . ."

"STOP!"

Again, her crackly old voice was sharp and stern. I was almost free except for one sleeve that still had thorns laced through it. But I froze, like she said.

The old woman walked a few feet away and picked up a long piece of driftwood from the bank. Then she came back. Instead of trying to get loose I just watched her.

"I don't mean to bother you," I said as she came nearer. "I just love animals. If you don't want me around, that's okay. But I'd at least like to watch. I mean you're great with animals. I won't bother nothing. I just want to . . ."

"Hush," she whispered.

She stepped beside me and reached down with the point of the stick. There, near my foot, was a snake. It was less than a foot away. It was a blackish-gray color and real thick. Gently, she eased the point of the stick under its belly and lifted it. Then she tossed it to the bank at the far edge of the thicket.

"You no belong here." She dropped the stick and glared at me. "You dumb kid. You get hurt, you keep coming here. Da bear eat you up. Turtles eat

you up. Water moccasin bite you. Even lime bush
eat you up. You go home!"

At last I was free from the thorns. She kind of
gave me a little shove toward the bridge. "You go
home and no come back."

"But . . . but . . ." I stammered.

She shoved me again. I made my way across the
one wooden board to the far bank. It was kind of like
walking a tightrope.

"Can't I just watch the animals? From over here?"

"Go home!"

Pouting, I turned and started up the path.

"You not just dumb, you stupid!" I heard her call
behind me. There was a different tone to her voice.
Somehow her piercing, crackly voice sounded almost cheerful.

"You be so stupid that you *do* come back, you
walk. No run! Only fool run from bear."

I nodded to the bear, gobbling down food from
the pan. "I woulda outrun him if I hadn't got stuck
in that darned thornbush."

The old woman cocked her head to the side.

"You outrun da bear 'cause you run downhill.
Bear not run too good downhill. You get lucky. You
run uphill, da bear make you look like you backin'
up. He so fast, he bite your bottom off and you not
even know it gone." She pointed up the hill. "You

walk home. Sing. Hum. Whistle. Make noise and *walk!*"

I pointed at the bear.

"He's so busy fillin' his stomach, I could do flips and he wouldn't notice."

The old witch just smiled. "Dis bear busy. Others come sometime, too. Dey maybe not so busy. You *walk!*"

The smile left my face and drooped clear down into my tennis shoes. I couldn't tell for sure if she was kidding about other bears. I didn't feel like taking any chances, though.

My eyes darted in every direction as I started home. When Mama opened the screen door for me, I was still humming and whistling as I stepped up on my back porch.

"Where have you been?" she greeted. "It's almost dark and . . ."

Suddenly, I heard her gasp.

"What on earth happened to you, Ted? Your clothes are torn. You're bleeding. You look like you got in a fight with a bobcat."

I glanced down at myself. I *was* kind of a mess. I wanted to tell Mama, "It wasn't a bobcat, it was a bear. But the bear didn't get me, because the witch saved me. Her lime bush got me but she helped me get loose and kept me from getting bit by a water moccasin. And there are turtles and bears and every animal under the sun out there."

But if I told Mama what *really* happened, she'd probably have a heart attack. So . . .

"I was playing down by the river," I lied. "I kind of got stuck in some briars. It doesn't hurt. I'm okay. Really."

I *was* okay, too. At least I was until Mama made me take my clothes off so she could doctor me. When she got the cotton balls and the hydrogen peroxide out and started dabbing all the little cuts and scratches, I wasn't okay anymore.

CHAPTER
18

"You're making it up," Jimmy scoffed.

"Am not."

"Are, too."

"Am not!" I protested. "There really was a bear and a water moccasin and . . ."

Don just sat there, pouting and playing with his mashed potatoes.

"That's a bunch of bull," Jimmy muttered as he stuffed a bite of chicken-fried steak into his mouth. "I bet you ain't never been out there again. Just that time when I went with you. There ain't no bears left in Louisiana. Even I know that."

The bell rang for recess. Jimmy and I jumped up to go dump our trays. Head hung low, Don shuffled along behind us. I guess I shouldn't have told Don and Jimmy. I only should have told Daddy. He would have probably been mad at me, but at least he would have believed me.

Don and Jimmy didn't.

Jimmy and I joined in the softball game. Don lay in the clover behind the wire backstop and didn't even watch. I didn't try to talk to either one of them again about the Witch of Blackwater Swamp. On the way inside for fifth-hour class, Jimmy invited us to come to his house after school or ride to the park.

We were at the door when he invited us. Don kicked the door open with his foot instead of reaching out to push it with his hand.

"Can't," he growled.

Jimmy and I looked at him, wondering why he was acting so cranky.

"How come?" I asked.

Don turned to glare at me.

" 'Cause somebody stole my new bicycle." His eyes seemed to cloud up. "We had one of those combination chains and had locked the bike on the back porch. Somebody cut the chain with somethin' and just took my bike."

"That's terrible!" Jimmy said, only there was something in his voice that sounded like he really didn't care.

It was terrible. Don loved that new bike. The last

time we rode to the park, he got a little scratch on the chain guard when he lifted it over the rock wall. I remembered how he almost cried. I hadn't known what to say, so I'd just stood there.

Don pushed his way through the door. "Daddy's talking about moving back to Austin. He's tired of having stuff stolen around here."

Jimmy cocked his head to the side and sneered. "Stuff don't get stole in Austin?"

Don glared at him. "Not like around here. Daddy says he's never seen a place like Lakeview. There's always someplace getting broken into or things being stolen."

Jimmy's eyes got wide. He shook his finger at Don and me. "I bet it's that old witch. She's always prowling around town at night, sneaking around in the dark."

I almost laughed.

"She wouldn't steal anything," I told them. "She just finds stuff for her animals—food or bandages or things like that."

Jimmy shook his head.

"Bet she does more than find stuff. Bet she steals stuff. She's black, ain't she?"

Frowning, Don and I both looked at him.

"So?"

Jimmy shrugged. "Well, you know how them

black people are. They're always stealin' stuff and lyin' and things like that. I bet she's the one doin' all this."

"That's the stupidest thing I ever heard," Don said. "There were a bunch of black kids in my school in Austin. They didn't steal stuff. They were nice."

"Yeah," I added, "and what makes you think you know so much about black people? Except for that old lady out in the swamp, there aren't any in Lakeview."

Jimmy smiled. His chest kind of puffed out.

"That's on account of Bubba and his friends. They keep black folks run out of Lakeview. This one family tried to move in about three years ago. There was a lot of stuff getting stole back then, too. Anyways, Bubba and his buddies nailed some wood together to make a cross and soaked it in gasoline and . . ."

Don and I looked at each other. Our eyes sort of rolled around. All we could do was shake our heads. We walked off and left Jimmy standing in the middle of the hall, talking to himself.

"Soon as Bubba and his friends run them black people out of town, the stealing stopped," Jimmy yelled down the hall at the top of his lungs. "There weren't no more stores broke into. Nothin' more got stole after they run them blacks out of town!"

Still shaking our heads, Don and I ignored him

and went on to class. Some of the other kids in the hall acted like they were listening. Don and I weren't.

Daddy had told me about prejudice, about how people didn't like or downright hated people who were a different color or who had a different religion or who were simply not the same as them. Jimmy was the first prejudiced person I'd ever run across.

I remember Mama worrying about moving to Louisiana on account of she'd heard that Louisiana and Mississippi were full of prejudiced people. Daddy assured her that she was wrong. He told her it wasn't just the South. He said that most of the people he'd met or worked with in Louisiana and Mississippi were good, honest, hardworking people.

"I've met enough prejudiced people in Oklahoma and Wyoming and even New York and New Jersey, to know that the South isn't the only place where people are like that," I remember him telling us. "There's places—all over the country—where somehow, ignorant and mean people just happen to get together."

After listening to Jimmy, I figured Lakeview just happened to be one of those places.

Then I remembered Mr. Parsons and my teachers and most everybody else in town. They weren't like Jimmy or his cousin, not at all. So I figured that maybe Daddy was wrong. Maybe it wasn't places at all. Maybe it was just dumb, nasty people that made it seem that way. Whatever . . . it was awfully complicated, and right now I had math with Mrs. Saxon. I quit thinking about it and trotted off to class.

"Daddy says he's gettin' sick of it, and so is everyone else in town." Don told us what else his dad had said when we met in the hall between fifth and sixth hour. "There's some kind of big meeting down at the courthouse tonight. Daddy says if the sheriff and the police chief don't get all the break-ins straightened out and stopped, *we're moving!*"

Jimmy shrugged. I wondered if Mr. Parsons knew about the meeting. I figured I'd stop by the store and tell him on the way home from school. Maybe Daddy would be home tonight. If he was, he'd probably like to know about the meeting, too.

Mr. Parsons already knew, and Daddy wouldn't be home until Friday. The next day at school, I found out that it was a good thing Daddy wasn't home. Mr. Parsons' store, Dr. Lyons's dentist office, and two houses that belonged to people who also went to the meeting got broken into that night. If Daddy had been home we would have probably gone to the meeting. Our house might have been broken into as well.

Don and I ate lunch alone that day. Jimmy was absent.

"We've moving," Don told me at lunch. "We're going back to Austin just as soon as Daddy can sell the house."

Guess that's why, the next day, when Jimmy asked me to ride my bike or come over and play with him, I said, "Sure."

With Don leaving and no one else to pal around with, Jimmy was the only friend I had. Like I've said before, Jimmy wasn't very nice. He said dumb stuff and he thought his cousin Bubba was the greatest thing in the world.

Even so, it was better than not having any friends at all. At least, that's what I thought.

CHAPTER
19

Jimmy came tearing up to the bicycle rack right after school.

"I got to stop by Connors for a minute on the way home. Let's go."

I remembered the last time I went to Connors, I'd promised myself I'd never go there again. Bubba and those two foulmouthed guys he hung around with were scary.

I dug around in my book bag for a minute.

"I forgot my English assignment," I lied. "You go ahead. I'll meet you at your house."

I left my bike and started toward the school building. But as soon as Jimmy rounded the corner by the playground, I closed my book bag and went back to my bike.

I rode slowly and kind of fooled around. But when I finally got to Jimmy's, he still wasn't there. I knocked on the front door to see if his mom was home. When she didn't answer, I leaned my bicycle against the garage and sat down in the field where we played.

Hard telling how long I sat there. It was more than long enough to know for sure that there weren't any four-leaf clovers in the little clover patch where I was sitting. Finally I got up and went to my bike, figuring that maybe Jimmy wasn't coming after all.

Then I decided I could get his ball and bat out of the garage. I could throw the ball up in the air and practice my hitting while I was waiting on him.

At the garage door, I hesitated. I remembered the day I went with him to get his baseball glove and how he said his mother didn't want anybody messin' around in the garage.

Then I remembered how he'd prowled through *my house* the time he spent the night. "What the heck?" I said. "How can he get upset with me for going into his garage when he explored our whole house?"

The big double, wooden garage door made a squeaking sound as I pulled on the right handle. It swung open, just enough for me to get my head through, then something stopped it. I tugged again. A chain held it at the top so it wouldn't open. Turning my shoulders sideways, I sucked in my tummy and wiggled my way into the dark garage.

It was pitch-black inside. I blinked a couple of times. Squinting, I waited until my eyes adjusted to the darkness. A small window, smeared and smudged with soap or paint, gave off the only light except for the tiny slit between the two doors where I'd slipped through.

Feeling my way along the door to the wall, I tried to find a light switch. There wasn't one. Finally, my eyes spotted a light bulb in the center of the room. I moved to it and waved my hand around under it, trying to find a cord or something. A string brushed my hand. After chasing it around in the air, I finally got hold of it and pulled. The light that flooded the room made me blink. My eyelids fluttered as I tried to adjust to the brightness.

When my eyes finally focused, I realized I'd never seen so much junk crowded into a garage before. Our garage was usually messy—at least if we stayed in a place for any length of time—but you could still get around. Jimmy's garage was the pits.

I realized how lucky I was to have made it to the light bulb in the center of the room. If I'd walked a little to the right, I would have tripped over the three motorcycles that stood there. A little to the left, and I would have gotten wrapped up in the row of bicycles. There were about seven or eight of them lined up, all together. I was lucky enough to hit the only path in the whole darned garage.

I looked around for Jimmy's bat and ball. I figured he had them hanging on the wall, like I did in my room. The walls were just as cluttered as the floor of the garage. There were shelves on three sides. The shelves were stacked high with boxes. There were radios and stereos, VCRs, cases of beer, and all sorts of junk. There was a book called *Scared Stiff*.

That's where my autographed book went, I thought to myself. I must have left it here when I spent the night . . . Then, with a jerk, I remembered that I'd never spent the night with Jimmy. I'd never been in the garage. The only way my book could have gotten here . . .

Suddenly, a chill raced up my spine.

It seemed to start at the very tip of my tailbone and bristle the little hairs at the back of my neck. Then it spread across my shoulders, arms, and clean out to the tips of my fingers.

Almost in slow motion, I turned back to look at the row of bicycles. Why would Jimmy have seven or eight bicycles? I asked myself. Why VCRs and cases of beer and . . .

The first bicycle in the row was brand-new. I walked to it and knelt down. There, on the chain guard, was a tiny scratch, a scratch left when someone lifted it over the rock wall at the park.

It was Don Lyons's bicycle, the bicycle that was stolen night before last!

My heart jumped up in my throat. It was pounding and throbbing so much, I couldn't seem to swallow.

My friend Jimmy was a thief!

In a daze, I staggered to my feet and headed for the door. I had to get out of here. I had to get away.

There was a big cardboard box near the door. Gasping for breath, I managed to get to it. I leaned against the box, kind of using it for support. Around the base, my eyes fell on a bunch of candy wrappers. I stared down.

LAKEVIEW ENGLISH DEPARTMENT FUND-RAISER

That's what the labels on the wrappers said. I remembered Mrs. Whitbeck making us stay in class while she tried to find out what had happened to Beth Farmer's candy bars. I looked inside the box I was leaning against. It was full of balls. There were basketballs and footballs and even dodgeballs. On one near the top, I read the label stamped into it:

PROPERTY OF LAKEVIEW ATHLETIC DEPARTMENT

On the shelf near the huge box were some smaller boxes covered with that fuzzy, felt stuff. A sick feeling rolled through my stomach as I remembered Mr. Parsons and that man talking about the break-in at Jake's Jewelry. I looked at the boxes of beer and whiskey. I remembered them talking about the liquor store break-in, too.

I was no longer in a daze. I no longer staggered or leaned against the box to hold myself up. In the blink of an eye, I charged for the door.

Slicker than a greased pig sliding under a fence, I slipped through the opening. I raced for my bike.

I had to get out of here!

I had to get home to Mama!

I had to . . .

A hand grabbed the front of my shirt. It lifted me up. I screamed. My legs, still running, kicked and jerked.

It was no use. The hand held me.

Eyes wide, I looked at it. On the arm, above the hand, I saw a tattoo. It was a blue picture of a devil with a knife stuck through its head. Drops of red ink poured from the skull like drops of blood.

Suddenly, Bubba Larkin's angry face was right in front of me. He was holding me so close that I could smell the cigarettes and beer on his breath.

"Where you think you're goin', punk?"

I kicked and struggled to get free.

Bubba's other hand went to my throat. His thumb and finger clamped down on either side of my windpipe. He squeezed. I couldn't breathe. I couldn't scream. He held on so tight, I couldn't even smell the foul stench of his breath.

"You ain't going no place." His evil eyes burned hot as he glared at me. "You ain't tellin' nobody nothing." He squeezed tighter on my windpipe. "You even think about telling, I'll rip your throat out and make you eat it!"

CHAPTER
20

There was a sharp pop sound from the other side of the big wooden door.

"It weren't my fault, Bubba," Jimmy whined. "Don't slap me no more."

"I done told you not to let nobody round this garage. I ought to . . ."

"It weren't my fault," Jimmy pleaded again. "If you hadn't made me hang around down at Connors to tell Deputy Russell that I seen the old witch coming out from behind the Lyons's house, I coulda got here 'fore he went to snooping around."

POP!

"Please, Bubba. Don't hit me no more!"

It was dark in the garage. When Bubba Larkin

dragged me back inside, he smashed the light bulb with his fist and threw me into the corner near the big cardboard box.

I wrapped my arms tight around my knees. I pulled them hard against my chest.

I cried at first. I felt like throwing up, both from him choking me and from the awful smell of his breath. I coughed and gagged.

How long I'd been sitting, shaking in the darkness, I don't know. It seemed like Bubba screamed and cursed at Jimmy forever. Jimmy kept whining and crying and swearing back at his cousin and telling him it wasn't his fault.

What they were going to do to me was too horrible to even think about. So I concentrated on listening to the voices on the other side of the big double, wooden door.

There was the sound of a car motor. Bubba and Jimmy stopped their screaming. The motor came closer. My eyes grew wide. Somebody was coming. Somebody who could help me.

I let go of my legs and lifted my chin from my knees.

If they got close enough, if I could hear someone talking, maybe I could scream. I could yell for help.

The sound of the motor stopped. It was close. I held my breath and listened. There was a woman's voice. It was too far away for me to hear what she was saying. She was coming nearer, though.

Maybe it was Mama. I shook all over. Maybe she had come looking for me. I crawled to my knees and took a deep breath.

"I told him it weren't my fault, Mom," Jimmy whined.

It was Jimmy's mother. I scooted against the door. She would help me. Moms always help people. She wouldn't let them hurt me. She'd . . .

She was close enough to hear, now.

The woman let out a string of curse words like I'd never heard before. It made the language Bubba and his friends used that day at Connors seem as tame as something you might hear at a church social.

I swallowed the deep breath I'd taken. It made my stomach tumble.

"I told you two that things were getting too hot," she growled at them. "But, no! You wouldn't listen. You had to break into houses and that @#*#&+# dentist's office. On top of all that, you let some dumb kid from school see the whole thing. How long's he been here?"

"About an hour," Bubba's sleazy voice answered. "What do we do with him?"

There was a long silence. I fell back against the box, shaking all over.

"Did you tell the deputy that story we made up about seeing the old black woman coming from behind the dentist's house last night?"

"Sure did, Mom," Jimmy answered.

"Tell anybody at school?"

"Yes, ma'am. Only a few people, just like you told me to."

"How about you, Bubba? Get any reaction from the guys that hang around Connors?"

I heard Bubba's evil laugh. "Sure did, Barbara."

"They buy it?"

"You bet. You know how dumb and stupid that bunch is. You could tell 'em the pope was Jewish, and they'd believe it."

Jimmy's mom let out with another string of curse words. "This messes up the whole plan. I figured it'd take a few days, maybe a week or so, for them to spread the word around town and get people stirred up. Then, we'd tell them that the old witch caught Jimmy when he was riding his bike and threatened to kill him if he told about seeing her sneaking round that dentist's house . . ."

I scooted closer to the doors. I leaned my forehead against the cold wood and peeked through a crack. I couldn't see heads or faces, just bodies. I saw a woman's hand go to Jimmy's shoulder.

"Bubba'd have to mark you up a little, son. You know, give you a black eye and a couple of scrapes, just to make it look convincing. That'd really get folks hot and bothered, some old black witch threatening to kill a white kid." She laughed. It was an evil sound. Then she cleared her throat. "But like I said, it'd take 'em a week or so to get mad enough to want to go do somethin' about her. That woulda give us time to move the rest of this stuff out and fence it in Shreveport." Her thumb motioned toward the garage.

"That dumb kid's messed the whole thing up. Now that he's seen all the stolen stuff, we don't have a week."

I could see Bubba's hand reach into the pocket of his blue jeans.

"I can shut him up!"

He pulled something from his pocket. It was blue, with silver on both ends. There was a "click" sound. A long, shiny blade sprang out.

It was a knife—a switchblade.

I pulled away from the crack in the wood. I was

shaking so hard, the box behind me started to rattle. The water welled up in my eyes.

"Put that up, stupid!" Barbara Weston's voice roared. "I got a better way of shutting that kid up."

Light flooded the garage. I pushed back against the cardboard box. I tried to melt into it, push myself so far into the corner that they couldn't see me.

It was no use.

"Grab him," Jimmy's mom snapped.

Bubba latched onto the front of my shirt. I tried to knock his hand away, but he was too big and strong. He lifted me to my feet.

"Sorry you got yourself into this mess, kid." She tried to make her voice sound soft and sweet, but there was a coarse, evil tone to her words. She nodded at Bubba.

With one quick jerk he spun me around, then wrapped his arms about me from behind. I was pinned. I couldn't even hit him.

I watched with wide terrified eyes as Jimmy's mom took a couple of battery-operated lanterns from a top shelf. She turned them on. Jimmy closed the door. Then, Mrs. Weston went to another box a few feet away. She pulled out a pair of plastic gloves. They were those thin, see-through kind that doctors and dentists use. She pulled one on. She turned to me, and wiggling her left hand into the other glove, she let go of the band. It made a popping sound when the plastic snapped tight around her wrist.

The smile on her face made her look exactly like the devil tattooed on Bubba's arm.

CHAPTER
21

"Nothing."

That's all I'd been able to tell Mama when she asked what was wrong. That's all I COULD tell her.

Mama knew there was something the matter. I guess that's why she kept asking me. My eyes were puffy and red from crying. She had wanted to know if I got in a fight with one of my friends.

I could only shake my head.

Finally, after asking me five or six more times what was wrong, she asked if I was sick.

I nodded, unable to answer her.

She took my temperature, gave me some aspirin, and put me in bed.

I couldn't sleep. I couldn't even close my eyes. The few times I did, I could see Barbara Weston's

evil face leering at me. I could see Bubba holding
me, and Barbara taking those rubber gloves and
picking up whiskey bottles and watches. One at a
time, she came back to where Bubba was holding
me and forced an object into my hands. Then, with
her plastic gloves, she'd take it and put it back on
the shelf.

It seemed like they made me hold or touch half
the stuff in the garage—VCRs, watches, rings, the
chrome on the bicycles, and the gas-tank lids on the
motorcycles. Finally, when they tired of it, Barbara
Weston told Bubba to let me go.

"Now," she said with that evil smile, "you got
your fingerprints all over everything. We use these
gloves. Our prints aren't on any of it."

She reached down and grabbed my chin. The
glove smelled funny.

"You tell anybody," she threatened, "we're gonna
tell 'em you helped steal it. They'll believe us, too.
All they got to do is check your fingerprints. You'll
go to jail. They'll take you away from your mama
and daddy and lock you up, if you tell."

I was scared to death. Still, somehow I managed
to glare back at her. I tried to be brave and
strong.

"They won't believe you." I made my voice
sound mean. "My mama knows where I am. You

steal stuff at night. She knows where I am every single night. They won't believe you."

That's when Bubba spun me around, then picked me up and held me. I was so close to him, my nose was almost in his mouth.

I gagged, nearly throwing up from the smell of stale cigarettes and old beer on his nasty breath.

"We'll get you and your family," he threatened.

"My daddy will kill you," I blustered. "He's big and strong and he'll . . ."

Bubba shook me so hard, I thought he was gonna break my neck.

"If we can't get your dad or you, we'll get your mother or"—his narrow eyes seemed to turn black—"or that cute little sister of yours."

I stopped struggling.

Bubba smiled.

"Yeah. We'll get her. You can't watch her all the time. Nobody can. Remember that night she was playing out by the road? You squeal, one of us will get her. If you get the cops on us, somehow, some way, some dark night, when you ain't even expecting it, one of us will get her."

The red numbers on the clock radio on top of my dresser said 1:30. I slipped out of bed as quietly as

I could. My legs trembled as I tiptoed down the hall.

I snuck to Kristine's bed and looked at her. In the glow from her night-light, I could see her face. She was sound asleep. Her little eyes were closed and her mouth was open with her breathing.

I put a hand to my nose and mouth, so my sniffling wouldn't wake her.

I never realized how much I loved my baby sister, how tiny and helpless she was. A tear dripped from my eye and plopped on the sheet next to her arm. Without a sound, I sat down on the floor beside her bed. Through cloudy eyes, I watched her sleep.

If anything happened to her, if anything bad happened to Kristine, I'd just die.

I didn't sleep at all that night. I did manage to get back to my room before Mama got up. I lay down and pulled the covers over my face. Mama looked in on me and in a few minutes, called me to breakfast.

When I came into the kitchen, her nose kind of crinkled up.

"You look terrible," she said. "I don't know what you have but I think you'd better stay home from school today."

I didn't argue with her.

She took my temperature, and when it registered normal, she scratched her head and put the thermometer back in my mouth. She made me take some aspirin anyway. At lunch she fixed me some chicken noodle soup. I didn't eat much of it, though.

About two, she peeked in to see if I was asleep. When I looked at her, she smiled.

"I've got a hair appointment," she said softly. "And a few errands to run. I'll take Kristine with me. You'll be all right while we're gone?"

I nodded and tried to smile.

In the other room, I could hear her shuffling around. I lay there, staring up at the ceiling, until I heard her keys jingle when she took them from her purse.

Suddenly, I kicked the covers back and leaped to my feet. From the living room, I heard the front door bang shut. I charged through the house and yanked it open, just as Mama was getting into the car.

"Watch Kristine," I yelled. "Watch her close. Don't let anything happen to her."

Mama frowned. Her head turned so far to the side, it almost touched her shoulder.

"Kristine and I have been to the beauty shop before," she said. "I'll take good care of her, just like I always do. Now you get back to bed."

I stood watching them until the car disappeared around the curve on the far side of the bridge. The screen felt cold against my cheek. I dragged myself to the TV and flipped it on.

After that, I tried to read a book.

After that, I cried some more.

After that, late in the afternoon, I put my clothes and shoes on, figuring some fresh air might make me feel better. The phone rang.

"Why weren't you at school today?" Don's voice was excited. "You sick?"

"Yes." I didn't lie to Don. I really did feel sick. I really was sick.

"Man, there was a lot going on today. You should have been there." When I didn't ask what happened, he went right on talking. "Jimmy Weston's got a black eye. It looks like somebody beat him to a pulp. You'll never guess what happened to him."

I nodded. I knew good and well what happened to Jimmy Weston. Only, I didn't dare say anything.

"He told everybody that the old witch caught him last night. You know, the old lady that lives out in the swamp? Well, he said he saw her sneaking around *our house* the night we got robbed! He said she caught him and said if he told anybody about it, she'd kill him or cast one of her evil spells on him.

Then she beat him up." He paused a moment. "Ted? You still there?"

"Yes," I whispered.

"Daddy said he'd heard about it, too. He says everybody who came to his dentist office today was talking about it. People are really upset. I mean, can you imagine some old witch beating up on a little kid?"

I wanted to tell him that the old woman wouldn't hurt a fly. I wanted to scream at him for being so stupid as to believe that lying Jimmy Weston. I wanted to tell Don . . .

I wanted to, but I couldn't.

I could only sit, holding the phone, and silently cry. I cried so much, my eyes hurt. My nose was sore and it stung when I touched it with a tissue or with the sleeve of my shirt. And like some dumb little kid, I cried some more.

"Gotta go," Don announced. "Dad needs the phone. Talk to you later."

I slammed the phone down. My fists squeezed so tight my whole hand turned white.

How could people believe such a lie? Why was it easy for them to fall for Jimmy's story? It made me so mad, I wanted to spit. How could anyone be that ignorant?

The sound of car horns yanked me from my anger. I shook my head and leaned to the side, listening.

There were motors and horns. I jumped up and raced to the front door.

Down the road, on the far side of the bridge, I could see some cars and pickups. There were five or six of them, almost like a parade.

The black '57 Chevy led the way.

The caravan stopped. Men started climbing out of the cars. Some jumped from the backs of the pickups. Though it was still light, they carried lanterns and flashlights. A couple had wooden torches with cloth tied around the end. The men moved to the middle of the bridge. One man brought a plastic can. He poured something on the wooden torches.

Then I could see Bubba Larkin.

He waved for the others to follow as he marched across the bridge to the little path that led into the swamp.

The icy grip of terror started at the tips of my elbows. It raced up my arms and met at my spine. It made me shudder.

They were going after the old woman, the old woman who did nothing but help poor hurt animals and who never bothered a soul.

I bit down on my lip.

For some reason, I remembered that day I ran from the bear. I remembered running into the lime bushes. Now, just like then, I was trapped. There was nothing I could do. I couldn't get away. I couldn't escape.

If I tried to stop the mob of men who moved across the bridge, Bubba and Barbara and Jimmy would get Kristine. They'd hurt her.

If I did nothing, if I just sat here, watching from the window, they'd get the old woman. Hard telling what this angry mob would do to her.

I hurt just like I did when I was stuck in the lime bushes.

Only this time the thorns weren't in my hands or my legs. The hurt that came now was like having thorns in the pit of my stomach. Thorns stuck right into my very heart, and I couldn't even cry.

CHAPTER
22

I guess it was the sound of Bubba's voice that yanked those thorns of fear and terror from me. It was that sleazy, slimy voice, the same voice and tone that had earlier filled my heart and soul with fear.

"Let's go get that old black witch!" he ordered. "She's been stealing this whole town blind."

Just short of the path, one of the men stopped. "Don't you think we should wait for the sheriff?"

Bubba turned to glare at him.

"After what she done to Cousin Jimmy? You see how she beat him up. Ain't nobody gonna get away with doin' that to one a my kin. I'm gonna go get her. Gonna run her clean out of the country. You guys with me?"

"Yeah," a roar went up from the mob.

"Let's go get her!" others shouted.

My churning legs carried me so fast, I was nearly across the backyard when I heard the screen door slam behind me.

Night was coming fast. Long shadows drifted across the path. The sun was nothing but a sliver of red above the horizon. I ran faster. I dodged stumps and ducked under limbs. A tree root caught the toe of my shoe. I stumbled but I didn't fall.

Cutting across my backyard had given me a good hundred to two hundred yard head start on the angry mob. Still, for a ways at least, I could hear their voices cursing far behind me. By the time I reached the place where the path left the riverbank and turned toward the forest, I had outdistanced them. There was no sound behind me.

Panting, gasping for air, I charged up the hill. That's when I heard it.

It was like the sound of a bell, only it was a deep, rumbling tone—more like a gong.

It came again and again, although I could barely hear it above my panting. I had run so hard and so long, my side hurt. I felt like someone was stabbing me with a knife. I forced myself to keep running.

My only chance was to get to the old woman
before the men did. I could warn her that they were
coming. I could get her away, and we could hide in
the tall grass or maybe even at the edge of the forest
above the ridge. If I could get to her in time, she
would be safe. If I could get there in time, Bubba
and his aunt would never know. They wouldn't try
to get back at me or my family if they never knew I
had helped or warned the old woman. If only . . .

I was almost in sight of the ridge that overlooked
Blackwater Swamp, but I couldn't run any farther.
My hands pressed against the pain in my side where
the hurt stabbed and gouged me. My teeth clinched
together so hard that I could feel my heart pounding
in my jaws and my temples. I dropped to one knee,
gasping for breath.

That's when I noticed another sound. Silence.
The crows, who always cawed at me with their
snotty little "caws," were quiet. Never, not once,
had I come near the forest without the crows shout-
ing at me. Not even a breeze rattled the leaves of
the trees. The sound of the "gong," the sound of the
old woman pounding the side of her black kettle
with the blunt end of the hatchet, even that had
stopped. There was nothing.

Still holding my side, I struggled to my feet. At
first I walked, then I began to jog. Finally, I ran. I

had to get there. I had to get the old woman away from the island before the men caught up with me. I ran and ran and ran and . . .

I gave a little skip-hop as I topped the ridge above Blackwater Swamp. In midair, I remembered the day I ran into the back end of the bear. I landed and dug my heels into the soft dirt, sliding to a stop.

The sun was gone now. There was nothing but an orange glow in the sky. Some clouds hung low in the west. The setting sun made them seem almost purple. I squinted, trying to see in the dim light. The path before me was clear. I charged down the hill.

The fading light cast an eerie glow across the swamp behind the old woman's house. The swamp grass seemed almost red, like ripples of blood that swayed and drifted with the waving grass.

"Old woman?" I screamed as I made the sharp turn at the bottom of the hill. I stopped running and walked along the bank, scanning the island for any sign of the witch. "Old woman. You got to get out of here. You got to run!"

When I heard no answer, I turned and walked quickly to the two boards that bridged the black water.

"Old woman! There're men coming. They're gonna hurt you! We got to get away!"

I was still watching the island, hoping to see her. Maybe she was in the cabin. Maybe she was tending the animals. I moved on, not watching where I was going.

"Where are you, old woman? Hey, old . . ."

I bumped against something. Then an arm wrapped around me. Held me tight.

Startled, I gasped. A black arm gripped my chest. A gnarled, wrinkled hand clutched my shoulder so tightly I could feel the long fingernails digging into my arm.

I looked up.

The Witch of Blackwater Swamp glared at me with black, angry eyes.

CHAPTER
23

I guess I was just too scared to be scared.

I know that doesn't make sense, but that's the only way I can describe how I felt.

And so, instead of struggling to get free or trying to run away, I wrapped my arms around the old, black, wrinkled arms that hugged me, and I hugged her back, as hard as I could.

"Why you come here, my child? Why you chest heave like wind-filled sail on small ship?"

I looked over my shoulder at her black eyes, her wrinkled face.

"You've got to get out of here," I pleaded. "There're men coming. They're mean and angry. I don't want 'em to hurt you."

Her smile looked almost soft in the evening light.

"I know men come," she said softly. "Animals tell me." With a wave of her arm, she motioned across the black water to her cabin.

I glanced around. The air stopped in my throat. There were crows everywhere. I guess I didn't notice them before because they were so quiet and still. Crows stood on the ridge at the top of her shack. They were as thick as a black feather blanket. I couldn't even see the brown boards. Crows clumped on the lime bushes and bent the limbs low. Crows sat on the cages where she kept her hurt or sick animals.

It was like that movie, *The Birds,* that Daddy had let me watch one night on TV. There were crows everyplace.

The sight made me shiver.

With a withered hand, the old woman turned me around to face her. "I know men come. Men come before. But why you come here?"

I was no longer out of breath. The words came tumbling and bouncing out of me like a broken string of pearls scampering down a wooden staircase. I told her all about Jimmy and Barbara and Bubba. I told her about the stealing and how they caught me and got my fingerprints all over stuff they'd stolen, and how they'd threatened me and

Kristine and how they'd made up this story so people would blame her and how they'd beat Jimmy up and told everybody she did it and how I was scared to do anything—until I saw the mob of men coming for her.

When I finished, I was panting. This time it wasn't from running, it was from talking so fast.

"You got to get out of here," I said once more. "You got to run away, quick! Go hide."

The old woman smiled at me and shook her head.

"No," she said softly.

"But . . . but the whole town's coming. They're gonna . . ."

She shook her head again. "No," she whispered, "not whole town. Just a few. Few stupid men with hearts that be so full of hate and fear, dey no have room for nothing else. Most town, okay. I no bother them, dey no bother me. Just a few."

"But you got to go. If they find you here . . . If they get hold of you . . ."

"No," she repeated. "Men like these come before."

A tiny gleam of light seemed to catch her left eye. It almost sparkled. "Dey think to find old woman who scared of dem. Find old woman who beg not to hurt her or burn shack. Dey think find old, helpless woman who all alone. But I be ready."

She turned toward the bridge. Her old, withered hand dropped to my elbow. She tugged.

I yanked away.

"No!" I pleaded. "There're too many of them. We got to run. We got to hide."

She glared at me, then shook her head.

"Dere be evil in dis old world." She sighed. "Best to stay away from it. Leave alone and hope it not come. But when da evil come to you, you no run away! You fight evil! You make da evil run. No other way."

She waved a wrinkled hand at the ridge. "Besides, too late to run away."

I glanced toward the ridge, expecting to see the glow from the men's lanterns. Instead, I saw the bear. It was the big black bear I had run into on the path. He lumbered slowly down the hill. Behind him, another bear—smaller than the first—followed.

"Evil men think old woman alone. Dey be wrong. Ole Witch of Blackwater Swamp have many friends."

She tugged me toward the bridge. I tugged back. "But if Bubba sees me . . . what about Kristine? They threatened to hurt her if . . . I've got to go."

The old woman practically dragged me to the

bridge. "You no go, now." She shrugged. "Da animals already here. Dey not know whether you good or bad. Dey maybe hurt you. Men come, too. Only place to hide is in cabin. Come—quick now." As we started across the bridge, she cautioned: "Walk only on right board."

Reluctantly, I followed her across the board on the right side. Once we were on the island, she picked up the metal bucket I'd seen her feeding the turtles from that first time I had spied on her.

She knelt at the edge of the bank and pounded the side of the bucket with a stick. Little heads began to pop up all across the surface of the black lagoon. She tossed some food to them, but not very much. Then she turned and led me by the hand.

At the door of her shack, she stopped. She picked up another bucket and, as I waited, took it to the far side of the lime thicket. She dumped something on the ground and tossed the bucket aside.

"Dere be bottle of lighter fluid on shelf inside door," she called. "You get for me, please?"

Cautiously, I opened the door of the shack and stepped in. It was bigger than I expected. At least, it seemed bigger than it had from outside. There was a little wooden bed near an open-hearth fireplace. At the head of the bed was a black chest or trunk. It had leather straps on it and brass handles. A wooden table and one chair were the only other pieces of furniture.

Shelves lined the walls. They were filled with bottles of medicine and bandages and cotton balls and all sorts of stuff for her animals. Two narrow shelves stood on either side of the fireplace. Those were filled with old books, some with leather backs, others so thick that it would take two hands to even pick them up. Frowning, I looked around on the shelf near the door. Sure enough, there was a bottle of charcoal lighter. I snatched it up and went outside.

The old woman pointed at the little pile of wood she had mounded up under the huge, black kettle. I squirted plenty of lighter fluid on the sticks, then snapped the top down and followed her into the shack. I put the bottle on the shelf where I'd found it, then turned to watch her. She got a match and went to light the fire. Once it was going she scurried back inside.

Almost trotting, she walked across the room to the big black chest with the brass handles. She dug around a moment and pulled out a long black dress.

"Not much time," she said. "Turn head, please."

I turned to face the fireplace. Behind me, I could

hear her clothes rustling. She grunted a time or two, like she was struggling with something.

"Okay, now," I heard behind me.

When I turned, she had pulled on a long black dress and was standing, with a smile on her face, in the center of the room. She put her tattered, brown dress in the trunk and pulled out a brush. Holding one strand of hair up at a time, she started brushing her hair, fluffing it up.

I'd seen Mama do that before. She called it "teasing her hair." It made my mother look like she had more hair than she really did. After she smoothed it down, Mama's hair always looked full and fluffy.

I shook my head. I couldn't believe it.

"Bubba Larkin and that whole bunch of men are coming . . . and you . . . you're brushing your hair. Why? What . . ." I stammered.

The old woman just smiled.

"They've got torches," I warned her. "They're gonna try and burn your cabin."

Nodding, she just kept brushing her hair and smiling.

"Da animals not let dem get close enough," she said. "If dey throw fire. . ." She pointed up at the roof with her hairbrush. "Crows not fly good at night. Dey throw fire—crows yell and scream and jump around and flap wings. Dey not fly away. Make fire go away."

"But . . . but . . ." I stuttered again. "Changing your clothes . . . doing your hair . . . What?"

She gave a little laugh.

"We see how dey feel when find old woman *not* alone. We see how dey feel when dey find bear and hungry turtles."

CHAPTER
24

It was dark in the cabin by the time the men topped the ridge above Blackwater Swamp. In the distance, I could see their flashlights and lanterns. I could hear their snarling voices.

The old woman had told me to stay under the bed. She had promised I would be safe.

I stayed there for only a moment. Then crawling on my hands and knees, I crept over to the wall. I leaned my forehead against the wood and peeked through a crack between the weathered boards.

I could see the lights moving down the path. They looked like a glistening waterfall trickling down a cliff. I couldn't see the old woman, so I scooted to a different spot. I moved into a corner of the room by the door. Wiggling around, I settled into the corner and found more cracks in the boards. If I leaned my head to the right, I could see the men and the bridge. If I moved to the left, I could see the old woman.

She stood beside the huge, black kettle. The glow from the fire beneath it cast ghostly shadows on her wrinkled face.

When she had finished "feathering" or "teasing" her hair, she didn't smooth it down like Mama always did. Instead, she left it sticking out in all directions. Her white hair spun about her head like some giant spider's web. The black dress she wore almost touched the ground. There was nothing in the black kettle, but the old woman held a long pole, about the size of a boat oar. She moved it round and round as if stirring something in the empty pot.

The wild hair, the black dress, the big kettle, the flickering firelight . . . With no wind to push the hot Louisiana air, it hung like a heavy blanket. Despite the heat, I felt an iciness that made me shake clear down to my toes. Right before my eyes, the old woman who loved and cared for animals and who would never hurt a soul became the Witch of Blackwater Swamp.

"There she is!" a voice called.

I leaned to the right, looking out the other crack between the boards.

The string of men who trailed down the path had stopped at the driftwood pile. Lights flickered and reflected across the smooth surface of the black lagoon.

"I see her," another voice answered.

The lights seemed to clump together as the men looked at her. Their angry muttering fell to silence.

The old woman screamed. It was a high, shrill, frightening sound. I looked quickly through the other crack. Like some lonely coyote, she leaned her head back and howled at the night sky.

The sound seemed to roll across the swamp. It raced up the hill. The haunting noise swept through the forest beyond the ridge. And when it finally drifted away on the still night air, an owl called. Then another and another.

For a moment, there was nothing but a frightening, empty silence.

"We're gonna run you clean out of the country." I recognized Bubba Larkin's voice. I leaned to the right so I could see. "You're gonna pay for what you done to my cousin Jimmy. You're gonna pay for all them things you done stole. And we're gonna fix it so you never do nothin' like that no more!"

I pushed my face into the corner so hard that I felt like I was going to get splinters in my nose. It was the only way I could see out of both cracks in the boards at once.

"Come to my island," the old woman taunted. Her voice was like the cackling of an old witch. "Come to me."

"We're gonna get you!" Bubba threatened.

"Come." She beckoned with a wrinkled hand. "Come."

The men were silent. Once they were quiet again, she began to stir the empty kettle. She began to chant, jumbling words together that didn't make sense. The words were from some strange language that she repeated over and over again.

Lights began searching the far bank of the lagoon. "There," someone said, "there's the bridge."

In line, the lights moved toward the two boards that crossed the black water. The old woman chanted louder. At the bridge, the lights stopped.

As my eye caught the old woman, I saw her drop an object that looked like a doll.

Suddenly, there was a loud BANG.

I closed my right eye and looked out my left. The little fire beneath the big black kettle flickered softly. From inside the kettle, a white ball of light and smoke puffed up.

When the smoke cleared, I saw the old woman. She held up another doll, made of straw and cloth. Chanting again, she waved it above the kettle, then dropped it in.

"Da spell is cast!" she shrieked at the men. "You will feel the water. It be cold—at first—then burn like da fire."

Again, a white ball of light exploded from inside the black pot. The white smoke covered the old woman like a fog.

She held up a third doll and waved it above the pot.

"I summon thee to my island. Da water awaits you. Cold water dat burns hot as fire. I summon da water. I summon da animals. Da animals who teeth are sharp, who belly are empty." She held the straw doll high in the air. "Three come. None leave."

With that, she dropped the third doll into the black kettle. This one didn't explode in a puff of white light. Instead a shrill, high-pitched, squealing sound came to the still night. It was like someone had taken a balloon full of air and stretched the opening tight. The high, shrill sound stung my ears.

"Butch. You and Charlie go get the old hag," Bubba's voice barked. "If she thinks she's a witch, we'll just dunk her in this here pond a few times." He laughed. "That's what they used to do back in

the olden days. We'll just see how long the old
witch can hold her breath."

Two flashlights shined on the wooden planks.
One of the boards creaked. Then the men stopped.

"How come you don't go get her yourself,
Bubba?"

There was no answer. In the dim glow from the
lanterns on the far bank, I could see Bubba. He
walked back to where the last two men stood in line.
He got the two sticks that I had seen them pouring
something on, back at the bridge. Another man
brought a lantern closer as Bubba dug around in his
pocket. He pulled out his cigarette lighter and
flicked it a couple of times. When the flame popped
out the top, he held it to the cloth.

Fire danced its way up the fabric. It swirled
around the cloth until the torch was aglow.

"I'll take care of her shack," Bubba boasted. "I'll
fire the cabin, and you drag her over here. Then
we'll all take care of her. We'll teach her not to mess
with the good decent white folk of Lakeview."

My teeth ground together inside my head. How
could Bubba Larkin talk about the good, decent
people of Lakeview? How could he even pretend
that he was doing something for somebody else? Of
all the sneaking, thieving, dirty, rotten . . .

"Well?" Bubba snarled as he brought the torch

and stood behind his two friends. "What you two waiting on?"

Cautiously, the two men stepped onto the boards. The others urged them on. Bubba moved up behind them. His torch burned brighter.

In the glow, I could barely see. The bridge was hidden behind the lime thicket. Then I saw something else—a couple of black lumps on the edge of the bushes. I squinted into the flickering shadows.

The bears!

I could hardly make out the two bears that the old lady had pointed to on the path when she told me it was too late to leave. They sat, hunkered behind the lime thicket, calmly munching the food she had dumped from the second bucket. They were so busy eating they didn't seem to notice the commotion on the other bank. The thicket hid them from the view of the men.

My eyes darted back to the bridge.

I remembered the day I ran across it. I remembered the old woman yelling: "Right board. Right board!" I remembered the cracking sound beneath my feet when the board snapped. I remembered how fast I was running, trying to get away from the bear, and how my speed had carried me to the far bank.

The two men on the bridge weren't running.

One step at a time, they moved across the boards. Their flashlights jiggled nervously in their trembling hands. And just as they were about halfway across the . . .

CRACK!

A flashlight went spinning through the air. A man yelled. He grabbed for his friend. Then there was a "splash" as both tumbled into the black water.

They were beyond the bears and the lime thicket, so I couldn't see them. But I heard them splashing around. They coughed and sputtered and slapped the water as they fought their way back to the surface.

"Dang, that's cold," one of them coughed. "Grab hold of the other board. Let's get out of . . ."

He never finished what he was going to say. A loud, agonized scream cut him short.

"Ouch!" his friend squealed. "What in the . . . AAHHH!!!"

"Somethin's got me!" the other man screamed. "It's killin' me . . . HELP! Help me!!!"

The men on the far bank scurried about. There were shouts and yells and above it all, screams of pain and agony from the two in the water. Everything moved so fast and furiously in the dim light, I couldn't tell what was happening. At long last, the splashing sounds stopped.

"Look at his leg," a voice quivered. "Look at that! Somethin' took a chunk, clean out of his leg. There's another. And there . . ."

"Look at Charlie!" a different voice came. It was so high and scared, it sounded like a little kid's voice instead of one of the men's. "He's got a chunk out of his side big enough to stick my fist in. Anybody got a handkerchief? A bandanna? We gotta stop the bleeding."

"It hurts!"

I could hear the pain and tears in the voice.

"It's burning. Somebody help me. Make it stop!"

Lights and men gathered around the two. Their voices were no longer angry. Instead, hushed, frightened whispers filled the night air like a soft, busy wind.

"We got to get 'em back. They need a doctor. I don't know what got hold of 'em, but we got to go get help."

There were mumbles of agreement. Then one angry voice snapped above the others.

"No."

The torch came back to the bridge. I could see Bubba. He stepped to the right board. He bounced up and down. When it held, he moved farther out.

"It's a trick," he barked. "The old woman set a trap for us."

He bounced again, testing the board at the center.

"It ain't gonna work, you old witch. Ya ain't scaring me off. Your little trap ain't gonna save you or your smelly old shack."

The old woman cackled again.

"Come! Come to my island. I tell you three come," she repeated.

How I got my thumb in my mouth, I don't know. I had my face pressed so hard into the corner of the shack—trying to see both directions at once—that there wasn't even room for my nose, much less my thumb.

But as I watched Bubba Larkin carry his torch across the wooden plank, somehow my thumb got in my mouth. I bit down on it. Chewed and chomped in a nervous frenzy until I was afraid I was gonna gnaw it clean off.

Once across the wooden board, Bubba Larkin marched boldly toward the old woman and her shack. Mean as ever, he waved his torch, cursing and calling out threats. Confidently, he marched beside the lime thicket and right into the two bears who were busily eating the food the old woman had left for them.

The smaller bear growled when he got beside

her. The big bear stood up on his hind legs and roared.

Even in the dark, I could see Bubba's eyes. They were as wide and white as the headlights on his '57 Chevy. The scream that came from his throat was more like a little squeak. The torch fell to the ground. Bubba spun and ran . . . smack-dab into the middle of the lime thicket.

It was strange, how the screams and squeals that came from Bubba Larkin reminded me of the third doll the old woman had dropped into the big black kettle. It was a sound like someone pinching the opening of a balloon, making the air squeak and sing as it rushed through the tiny opening.

Bubba kept screaming and squalling and struggling against the long sharp thorns. The harder he fought, the more the long spines dug into him and held him tight.

"We got to get him," one of his friends ordered. "Come on."

"But . . . the bears . . ."

"Get me that other torch. They're afraid of fire. I'll hold 'em back with the torch, you get Bubba."

The old woman held up another doll.

"Who be next?" she called out. "Who come to da island of da witch?"

A flashlight broke from the crowd of men and bounced up the hill.

"Forget you!" a voice called. "I'm getting out of here!"

"What about Bubba?"

A second flashlight broke from the group.

"Forget Bubba, too," another whined. "This whole thing was his idea. He got himself into this. Let him get himself out. I'm goin' home!"

An explosion of movement erupted on the far bank. Lights scampered around. The two hurt men pleaded for help. Some of their friends grabbed them and all scurried toward the top of the ridge. Above the running feet and pleas for mercy, I could hear Bubba yelp and whine as thorn after thorn dug into him. And above the sound of his screams, I could hear the old woman's laugh.

Only, it wasn't really a laugh. It was a cackle. A cackle that only the Witch of Blackwater Swamp could make.

CHAPTER
25

When the men were gone, the old woman came back to the cabin. She had me follow her out the door and cling close to the wall until we were on the far side of the cabin. Once there, I followed her to the edge of the island. She knelt and felt around in the darkness until she found a rope tied to a log. She began pulling. A soft rustling sound made me glance toward the marsh grass. A small boat slipped from its hiding place in the tall weeds and glided through the shimmering moonlight that danced on top of the black water.

With a finger to her lips, the old woman shushed me and motioned to the bottom of the boat. "I take you home. Too dangerous to go by self at night," she whispered. "But we need hurry. You hide so nobody see. I go make sure da dumb man in bush still be here when get back."

Quiet as I could I climbed into the boat and sat down while she scurried toward the lime bush.

"If not be still," I heard her caution Bubba, "da bears gonna eat you. I come back, either find you be very still in bush or find bear with fat tummy."

She brought a long pole with her when she returned from the cabin. Shushing me again, she had me lie down in the bottom of the boat. Quiet as a dewdrop forming on a blade of grass, she used the pole to shove the boat away from the island and into the swamp grass. Once there, she let me sit up, but we were well away from the island before she would let me speak.

"You don't really think the bears will eat Bubba, do you?"

"No," she answered with a sly smile. "Give da bears special treat—bologna and strawberries and grape jelly in da bowl. Why dey wanna eat somethin' as stinky and ugly as Bubba when got bologna and strawberries? Dey not bother him lessen he scare 'em. He not scare 'em. He be real quiet."

Without a sound, the boat slipped from the cover of the swamp grass onto the open, still water of the river. Using the long pole, she kept us near the far bank and moved quickly downstream.

I didn't even realize how tightly my fists were clenched, until I felt my fingers begin to tingle. I flexed my hands and looked back at the old woman. "Bubba's gonna know I told you, I helped you."

"How Bubba know? He still in bush."

"His friends will see us when we get to the house. They'll see the boat and see you and me and know that . . ."

"Men see nothing but place where feet step," she interrupted me. "You be home in bed and I be back on island before dey get dere."

With a crooked finger, she motioned across the river. I could see the glow of flashlights moving single file down the hill toward the riverbank. The noise from feet snapping branches and twigs sounded like a herd of elephants walking on egg-shells.

"I'm gonna die," a quivering voice whined. "I'm bleeding to death."

"Ah, shut up," another voice grumped. "You ain't hardly bleeding anymore. Few stitches and you'll be good as new."

"But I'm bleeding. It hurts! Hurry, please."

"Shut up! We're walking as fast as we can. It ain't easy carrying you through this jungle."

Their voices and the racket they made crunching through the brush faded behind us as the old woman

slipped the boat through the still water. In the daylight, it took me twenty to thirty minutes to make
the walk from our house to the witch's island. On
the river, it took only ten minutes to get home.
Mama must have had every light in the house on. It
shined like a beacon from across the dark river.

"Mama's gonna kill me," I sighed. "I bet she's
worried sick."

The old woman slipped the boat next to the bank
and lay the pole across it. "Dere be other men like
Bubba and his friends," she told me. "It be best if
people not hear what you see happen tonight."

"Why?"

"Lot of men come to scare one old woman. Instead, one old woman scare dem and make dem
run away. Dey have to make up big story about
how powerful old witch be and how mean and evil
she is. By time dey carry hurt friends back home,
story get bigger and bigger. When tell story,
nobody else want to mess with Witch of Blackwater
Swamp.

"You tell of dolls stuffed with chemicals I find in
trash cans, tell dat just big turtles bite men in water
and bears only come to fill fat tummy with grape
jelly—dat not so scary. Best let dem make up
gooder story."

She waited for me to get out. I didn't. Mama

would be furious at me for leaving the house and not coming back until so long after dark. In fact, I was probably in so much trouble, I never would be able to get out of it. She'd never believe me, but if both of us . . .

"Tell you what." I smiled. "I'll make a deal with you. I won't tell how you scared those men off your island if you'll come and tell Mama where I was and . . ."

"NO!"

Mama *was* mad at me, all right. What with all the cars parked by the bridge and me not being there and her not knowing what was going on, she was in a total snit when I sneaked in the back door. She cried and hugged me. She yelled and scolded and cried some more and hugged me again. Then she told me I could never leave the house by myself, *ever again*, and that I was grounded for the rest of my life. And, finally . . .

She looked past me to where the old woman suddenly appeared from the shadows beside the back steps. Mama stopped talking and her mouth flopped open. Her eyes got big around as two eggs frying in a skillet.

"I am Martha Timms," the old woman said. "Your

son has been wit me. He come to protect me from men dat try to burn my cabin and hurt me."

Mama made a gulping sound when she swallowed. Martha Timms smiled.

"May I come in?"

Kristine didn't know about witches or any stuff like that. She was too little. All she knew was that a lady with a soft voice was sitting in our living room.

So, being too little to listen to scary stories or to know about such things, Kristine saw the Witch of Blackwater Swamp for what she really was. No sooner had she sat down than Kristine trotted over and climbed in her lap.

It made Mama a little nervous.

Kristine wasn't the least bit worried, though. She played patty-cake with Martha Timms while I told Mama about what had happened to me when I stumbled onto all the stolen stuff in the Westons' garage. Then as the old woman told Mama about what had happened tonight, Kristine lay her little head against the witch's shoulder and smiled at the soft, flowing sound of the voice.

Kristine was fast asleep by the time we finished. The old woman gently handed her to Mama, who put her in bed, then came back to the living room.

Martha made a grunting sound when she got up from the couch. "Hope you not be too mad at da boy," she told Mama. "He brave boy. Good boy."

"I didn't do anything." I shrugged. "You already knew the men were coming. You took care of them, you and the animals. I didn't even help. I just . . ."

"You do da right thing. You learn not be scared of bad people like Bubba and not listen to threats dey make. You risk you own safety to do what be right. That be enough. Dat be more dan most grown men able to do."

There was a loud rapping sound of someone knocking at the door. All three of us jumped.

Mama glanced at the door, then back at us. "Must be Sheriff Thibodeaux. I was so worried when I couldn't find Ted, I finally called him." She glanced down at her watch. "He said he'd be here as soon as he could."

The old woman took a step toward the back of the house, then stopped.

"Sheriff Thibodeaux be good man," she told Mama. "But he not need to know dat boy have any part in what happen. You tell him boy come home right after you call. Ted, you say you see men walking upriver and follow, but get scared of dark and hurry home. Say you come home right after Mama call him."

She moved toward the kitchen. The knocking sound came again.

"But what about all the stolen stuff?" I called after her in a whisper. "How's he going to know about all that if I don't . . ."

She smiled.

"Bubba tell him."

I frowned.

"Huh?"

"Bubba tell him," she repeated.

I shook my head. "Bubba would never do that. He's too sneaky . . ."

"Bubba tell him." She winked at me. "Maybe have to have talk with bear first, but Bubba tell. One thing bear like better dan grape jelly, dat be honey. Believe me, Bubba gonna tell sheriff *everything!*"

The knocking sound came, one last time. I glanced at the door for only a second. When I turned around, the Witch of Blackwater Swamp was gone.

We stuck to the little white lie, just like the old woman asked us to. Sheriff Thibodeaux asked me about the men, like how many and who they were. But before I could answer, another knock came at our door.

Mama opened it and one of Sheriff Thibodeaux's deputies stood there. He tipped his hat and looked past her to where the sheriff was sitting on our couch.

"Anthony, you best get out here," he announced. "That old witch, who lives out in the swamp, just come up to the bridge in a boat. She says she's got Bubba Larkin out to her shack. Told me to tell you to hurry before one of her animals eats him and gets sick."

Sheriff Thibodeaux excused himself and scurried off after the deputy. Mama closed the door and we hugged each other so tight, I thought my eyes were going to pop out of my head.

Lakeview turned out to be a pretty nice town, without Bubba Larkin and Barbara Weston. They went to trial about six months after the men went to the island. What with Bubba's signed confession and Sheriff Thibodeaux's testimony, it wasn't much of a trial though. They both went to prison. It was hard to find out anything about Jimmy. Word at school was that Bubba told the sheriff that since Jimmy was so small they would squeeze him into the air conditioner vents. They could steal things and leave no trace of a break-in. Talk had it that Jimmy spent a few months in Juvenile Hall, then went to California to live with an aunt. Nobody really knew for sure, though.

So like I said, Lakeview turned out to be a pretty nice town. Except for the small group that hung around down at Connors and told terrifying stories about the old Witch of Blackwater Swamp, most of the people were pretty nice. I made some good friends there. Two years later, when we moved to New Mexico, I really hated to leave.

Hanging around with Don Lyons finally got me hooked on books. When I packed, I took my Nintendo to the trash. It was old and beat up, anyway. Besides, there wasn't room to pack it with all the books I had collected.

One of the best books I had was an old, tattered book about animals and the medicines that could be used to cure them when they were sick. It was a big book. I had to use both hands just to pick it up. It had a leather back on it that was cracked and weathered. It smelled of smoke from the open fireplace in Martha Timms's shack. I'd learned a lot about animals from that old book. I'd learned even more from the Witch of Blackwater Swamp.

The memories of her, the animals, and the book would always stay with me.

*   *   *

One of Daddy's prized souvenirs was the picture. In fact, he wouldn't even pack it. He was scared the glass frame might get broken, and he didn't want it damaged in any way.

When we got in the car and backed out of the driveway, I shrugged at the For Sale sign in our front yard. Then I glanced down at the picture that Daddy had put on my lap. I would hold it all the way to our new home in New Mexico. It was my job to make sure nothing happened to it.

It was a picture of a giant alligator snapping turtle. The thing was huge. Its beak was more like some giant dinosaur than like a turtle. A mountainous ridge ran down the center of its shell with two little ridges beside it. It lay half hidden in black water. In the background was a rickety wooden shack. And standing next to the shack was an old woman. I could barely make her out.

She stood in the shadows. She was as black as the night, with white hair that was as wild and free as the clouds.

She was Martha Timms.

She was the Witch of Blackwater Swamp.

She was smiling.

ABOUT THE AUTHOR

BILL WALLACE was a principal and physical education teacher at an elementary school in Chickasha, Oklahoma, for ten years. Recently, he has spent much of his spare time assisting his wife coach a girls' soccer team. When Bill's not busy on the soccer field, he spends time with his family, cares for his five dogs, three cats, and two horses, lectures at schools around the country, answers mail from his readers, and of course, works on his books.

Bill Wallace's books have won fourteen awards and made the master lists in twenty-two states. *Beauty* (winner of the Kansas William Allen White Award and the Oklahoma Sequoyah Award); *The Biggest Klutz in Fifth Grade; Buffalo Gal; The Christmas Spurs; Danger in Quicksand Swamp* (winner of the Pacific Northwest Young Readers' Choice Award and the Maryland Children's Book Award); *Danger on Panther Peak; A Dog Called Kitty* (winner of the Nebraska Golden Sower Award, the Oklahoma Sequoyah Award, and the Texas Bluebonnet Award); *Ferret in the Bedroom, Lizards in the Fridge* (winner of the Nebraska Golden Sower Award and the South Carolina Children's Book Award); *Snot Stew* (winner of the Texas Bluebonnet Award and the South Carolina Children's Book Award); *Never Say Quit; Blackwater Swamp;* and *Totally Disgusting!* are available from Minstrel Books. *Trapped in Death Cave* (winner of the Florida Sunshine State Young Readers' Award, the Utah Children's Book Award, and the Wyoming Soaring Eagle Book Award) and *Red Dog* are available from Archway Paperbacks.